THE CAERPHILLY MOUNTAIN KILLINGS

A gripping murder mystery

GAYNOR TORRANCE

Jemima Huxley Crime Thrillers Book 3

Originally published as *Stalked*

JOFFE BOOKS

Revised edition 2022
Joffe Books, London
www.joffebooks.com

First published by Sapere Books in Great Britain
in 2020 as *Stalked*

This paperback edition was first published
in Great Britain in 2022

Cover art by Nebojša Zorić

ISBN: 978-1-80405-285-3

PROLOGUE

For urbanites, the reality of life in the countryside might be far removed from the romantic idyll they often yearn for. What is tranquil during the day becomes isolating at night, when darkness can feel oppressive, palpable and thick as tar. If you come unprepared for the experience, there's a chance it can mess with your mind.

The abductor and the victim had reached the middle of nowhere, with only nocturnal creatures aware of their presence. Street lighting was non-existent on the winding country lane. The vehicle jolted as one of its wheels hit a pothole in the road. The driver cursed and gripped the steering wheel even tighter.

Slumped forward, slack-jawed and dribbling, Violet Watkins's chin struck her chest, forcing her teeth to snap together as they broke through the surface of her tongue. She was too far gone to appreciate what had happened, oblivious to pain of any kind.

As the car came to a halt, a movement sensor bathed the immediate area in bright artificial light. The driver switched off the engine, got out and opened one of the vehicle's rear doors, before reaching in and feeling for the button to release Violet's seatbelt.

With knees bent, and feet spread, the abductor clamped Violet's midriff in a vicelike grip as she was hauled out of the vehicle and dropped unceremoniously into a rusty wheelbarrow. Violet landed with a dull thud and lay in a crumpled heap. Blood trickled from her mouth.

Moments later, the wheelbarrow was forced across a bed of chippings, creaking loudly as the wheel turned. The stones crunched and moved, releasing small puffs of dust along the way, until the smooth flagstone floor of a building allowed the wheel to turn freely.

Once inside, Violet was hauled up a narrow staircase and dragged into one of the two rooms, before being tossed on to a bare mattress on a metal bed frame.

Cotton pads were placed over her eyes, secured in place with duct tape. It was an unnecessary precaution — there was no intention of allowing her to leave the room alive. Restraints, already fixed to the metal frame, were fastened around her wrists, ankles and neck, allowing little freedom of movement. Not that they were required, until the effects of the drug wore off.

PART ONE: 2019

CHAPTER 1

Detective Inspector Jemima Huxley was deep in conversation with Chief Inspector Ray Kennedy and Detective Sergeant Dan Broadbent when her phone rang.

'I should get this,' she said, reaching out for the handset and grabbing a pen.

'There's a man on the line, asking to speak with you. Sounds rather upset,' DC Gareth Peters told her, before hanging up to allow the call to come through.

Jemima hadn't had time to draw breath before an agitated voice was almost shouting at her. 'DI Huxley?'

'Yes, that's right. Who is this?'

'You don't know me. But you know my wife — Violet Watkins.'

The mention of the woman's name sent a shiver down Jemima's spine. It was a name she had done her best to forget. A name she hadn't heard or uttered for six years. 'Violet Watkins?' she repeated, in an attempt to confirm that she hadn't misheard. As she felt the colour drain from her face, she saw Broadbent leap to his feet and Kennedy stiffen in shock, a mug of coffee inches from his open mouth.

Violet had first come to their attention six years earlier when a man named Byron Toombes became fixated on her.

It had been a steep learning curve for everyone, as it was their first encounter with a stalker. Even DCI Kennedy, who, with years of experience under his belt, believed he had seen everything the job could throw at him, felt out of his depth. As hard as they worked to try to pin something on Toombes, they were unable to obtain sufficient evidence to make anything stick. Hardcore villains were one thing, but when you were up against a stalker, you soon began to realize that it was impossible to predict their next move. And at times it had felt like they were trying to stop the Terminator. It was an unusual and extreme mindset to get to grips with — someone so focused on a particular objective that they were content to obliterate anything standing in their way.

There had been no second-guessing what Toombes was capable of. He proved his resourcefulness and resilience in his relentless pursuit of Violet. Anyone who happened to get in the way became collateral damage, and some paid a heavy price indeed.

Despite doing everything in their power to protect her, they all felt that they had let Violet down. Throughout the investigation, Jemima and Broadbent had gone above and beyond as they attempted to bring Toombes to justice. But the law constrained them and events conspired against them, thwarting the police at every turn. What had started as a battle of wills soon became a game of cat and mouse, with many surprises along the way.

The case pushed everyone to their limit, as Toombes's determination never wavered. At the end of it, Broadbent almost died, Jemima was seriously injured, and Violet's outlook on life would never be the same again.

When they realized that this phone call was about Violet, the chief inspector was the first to recover. 'Put it on speakerphone,' he demanded, before cursing in a hushed tone as some of his hot coffee slopped over the mug's rim and landed on his trousers.

DS Finlay Ashton had sauntered into the room but stopped abruptly when Kennedy held a hand up.

'I'm putting you on speakerphone. Give me your name and tell me what's happened,' said Jemima.

'I'm Charlie Morgan. My wife, Violet, has gone missing. I know that you worked on the case six years ago.'

'I thought Violet had moved away from Cardiff?' said Jemima.

'She did, but we returned about two years ago. I thought she'd be safe. There'd been no sign of Toombes in all that time. We checked with South Wales Police before we moved back and were told that he was still missing. So I convinced Violet that she was at no greater risk here than anywhere else. In fact, I thought it may be safer for her in Cardiff as he was hardly likely to return. Look, this isn't helping. You need to find her!'

'I appreciate your concern, Mr Morgan, but before we can do anything I need to know exactly what has happened,' said Jemima.

'Yes, yes, sorry. I'm just so worried that I can't think straight at the moment.' He took a deep, shuddering breath before continuing. 'Violet went out last night with some of her work colleagues. She never made it home. I returned this morning after pulling an all-nighter — I head up a team at the National Crime Agency. Because of the operation, I had my phone on silent throughout the night. Violet left me a message saying that she was on the bus and she'd be home by eleven. She's obsessively cautious. Naturally so, after everything that happened back then. But when I arrived home this morning, there was no sign of her. Our bed hadn't been slept in. She never makes the bed, and she sure as hell wouldn't stay out all night. Something's happened!'

'Try and stay calm,' said Jemima. 'You don't know that for sure.'

'Yes, I do. Violet was with her friend Beth. They were both on the bus, but I've spoken with Beth's partner, Anton, and he said that she didn't make it home either. I've already rung around the hospitals, but neither of them was admitted. Anton's driving around looking for them as we speak. I told him that I'd get in touch with you.'

'As you're with the NCA you know the drill. Given her history with Toombes, we'll treat Violet's disappearance as a priority. Let me have your address, and we'll be right over.' As Jemima spoke the words, she turned to look at Kennedy, who nodded his agreement.

'If it turns out to be Toombes, are you sure you two are up for this?' he asked, addressing Jemima and Broadbent.

'Definitely.' Jemima nodded determinedly and glanced towards her sergeant.

'Yeah, let's get the bastard,' said Broadbent, in a tone that failed to match the words he'd uttered.

'Are you going to tell us what's going on?' asked Peters.

PART TWO: 2013

CHAPTER 2

Jemima had recently joined Detective Inspector Ray Kennedy's major incident squad in Cardiff as a newly appointed sergeant. She'd worked hard to make it through the promotion process, putting in the hours, consistently doing far more than was asked of her. There had been many a night when she had survived on less than six hours' sleep. But she was career-driven, determined to succeed and well aware of the need to prove her worth. So far, her work ethic had paid off, but she knew that in itself wasn't enough to ensure progression in a male-dominated workplace.

Despite being as good as, if not better than, many of her male colleagues, Jemima realized how fortunate she was. It had been a speedy career progression, and the fact hadn't gone unnoticed by others on the force. She had been awarded an almost perfect score in her sergeant's exam and had aced the interview — a result achieved through self-discipline and a lot of hard work. Although Detective Inspector Ray Kennedy had welcomed Jemima with open arms, she hadn't counted on the simmering resentment of Detective Constable Daniel Broadbent. She had heard it said that he had expected the sergeant's post to be his, though she couldn't understand why he had thought it was a given. It was an open secret that

Broadbent had failed the sergeant's exam and so hadn't even reached the interview stage.

At the time of Jemima's arrival, DC Broadbent had worked with Kennedy for almost five years. Broadbent was a decent enough police officer, despite being a bit lazy. Those who knew Broadbent described him as genial, though, so far, Jemima hadn't seen that side of his personality.

Early that morning, Ray Kennedy strode up to Jemima's desk. As a rule, he didn't often venture out of his office. And on this occasion, he had the look of someone who was troubled.

'Huxley, a word in my office, now,' he said. His tone was severe, and the words clipped.

As Jemima followed Kennedy out of the room, she was surprised to see Broadbent smile at her. She returned the smile, all the while puzzling over why there seemed to be such an unanticipated thaw in hostilities.

'Come in, Huxley. Shut the door and take a seat.' Kennedy made himself comfortable in his chair. 'I've had some troubling news I want to share with you.'

Jemima's mind raced ahead. Kennedy wanted to talk to her in private, and Broadbent had appeared smugly satisfied. It didn't bode well.

'My wife is a district nurse, and the husband of one of her patients, a circuit judge, asked to be put in touch with me. Apparently, his granddaughter is having trouble with her next-door neighbour.'

'I'm sorry, sir, but I don't understand what this has to do with us?' said Jemima, with a puzzled expression on her face.

'I didn't either, but it seems that this is no run-of-the-mill spat. The judge refused to go into specifics over the phone. The only thing he was prepared to say is that the man in question — Byron Toombes — is a scene-of-crime officer working alongside our police force. Judge Douglas Pickering is presiding over a case at the Crown Court next door. He'll be adjourning for lunch at midday, when he intends to apprise us of the situation.

'I'm sure I don't need to remind you of the sensitivity of this matter. If what the judge tells us warrants an investigation, it will need to be handled with alacrity and care. Given the links to this force, it's essential to keep the circle close, so as not to compromise any potential investigation. Not a word to anyone. We'll leave the building separately, and I'll meet you inside the Crown Court building shortly before midday.'

'Everything OK?' asked Broadbent, as Jemima returned to her desk.

'Yes,' said Jemima. It was evident that Broadbent was fishing for information, but she wasn't going to betray Kennedy's confidence.

CHAPTER 3

Jemima was already in the reception area of the Crown Court when Kennedy walked in.

'I've already asked for directions,' she said. 'Apparently, Judge Pickering left instructions for us to go straight through to his chamber.'

'Let's get a move on,' Kennedy replied. 'After all, we don't want to run the risk of bumping into anyone we know.'

'It seems very cloak and dagger.'

'That's as maybe, but Pickering was very clear that he wants to keep the circle close on this. Until we've spoken to him, and found out what's going on, I'm of the mind that we must respect his wishes,' said Kennedy.

The corridor they set off along took them to an area of the court that they were both unfamiliar with. Like the majority of the buildings in the Cathays Park area of Cardiff, the structure was somewhat dated. Judge Pickering's room was at the far end, and as the door was closed, Kennedy knocked and listened for a response. As none was forthcoming, he opened the door, and they both stepped inside.

The room was far smaller than Jemima had anticipated. More oversized cupboard than a grand office space befitting a judge. It was situated away from the outside of the building and lacked any natural light, which would have given the room a bigger feel. An air-conditioning unit rumbled away in the background, located somewhere above the false ceiling. Everything about the space suggested outdated grandeur. There was a great deal of mahogany furniture and wall-panelling, which sapped what little artificial light there was. It was oppressive, somewhat shabby and smelt slightly musty. The far wall was filled entirely by a built-in bookcase, crammed with leather-bound tomes, providing the room with its only significant splashes of colour.

On top of a large mahogany cabinet stood a tray of refreshments — assorted sandwiches, a bowl of fruit, a large bottle of mineral water, a thermos jug, three glasses, three mugs, milk and sugar.

Jemima smiled. It seemed that Judge Pickering had thought ahead.

The door opened and the judge entered the room.

Douglas Pickering was a tall, willowy man, with sunken cheeks, a bald head and piercing blue eyes. For someone so slim he had a firm handshake. His voice was deep, and the gravitas implicit in his tone immediately commanded respect. Jemima had not been called upon to give evidence in any case he had presided over, but the few moments she had spent in his company gave her the immediate impression that this man would not stand for any misbehaviour in his courtroom.

'Detective Inspector Kennedy and Detective Sergeant Huxley,' said Kennedy, as he held out his hand to the judge.

With the introductions out of the way, they sat down to listen to what the judge had to say.

'As I mentioned on the telephone, I'm rather concerned about my granddaughter's wellbeing,' Pickering began. 'You can see from this photograph that she's an attractive young woman.' He opened his briefcase and extracted a snapshot of her. 'Her name is Violet Watkins.'

'I think I know her,' said Jemima. Her brow furrowed as she tried to recall where she had seen the young woman before.

'Oh, I doubt that,' said Pickering.

'Was she an undergraduate at Oxford?'

'Yes. Were you?'

'No, but my sister was, and I think they're friends.'

'I'm afraid I wouldn't have any idea about that. As a grandparent, I don't get to socialize with Violet's contemporaries. Anyway, I digress. Let's focus on the reason I asked you here. About four months ago, Violet relocated to Cardiff, when she took up a post here. She's the sort of girl who could turn her hand to anything. After all, Oxbridge opens many doors. I had high hopes that, after graduation, she'd go on to have a stellar career in one of the many prestigious companies around the globe. But it wasn't to be, as she's developed a social conscience. My granddaughter's an altruistic idealist, always seeing the best in people — a seemingly rare commodity these days. Ultimately it came as no surprise when she was head-hunted for a senior role at an NGO.

'When we heard about the location of the post, my wife and I offered to take her in. But being young and single-minded Violet turned us down, opting instead to rent a terraced property not far from the city centre. Apparently, it's in one of the up-and-coming areas, whatever that means. She rented the property through a reputable agency, which manages the let on behalf of the owners.

'I've no complaints about the property, but what concerns me is the next-door neighbour. As I've already told you, his name is Byron Toombes. He's considerably older than Violet, and from what I've been able to establish, he has been pestering her. According to Violet, she hasn't encouraged him in any way, but he isn't prepared to take no for an answer.'

'If I could stop you there, Judge Pickering,' said Kennedy. 'You, more than most people, must appreciate that the things you've told us about are not criminal matters. Has this Byron Toombes threatened your granddaughter, or given her cause to fear for her safety?'

'No, as far as I'm aware, he hasn't. But I'm confident that there's more to it than Violet is prepared to tell me. So

I was hoping that you would both do me a personal favour and perhaps Sergeant Huxley could go and have a word with my granddaughter? I'm sure she'd be more inclined to open up to another woman, especially a female closer to her own age. I have an ominous feeling about this chap.'

'And the only thing you know about him is that he's a scene-of-crime officer working with this police force?' asked Kennedy.

'Yes, which if I'm right makes it even more likely that he'll tamper with any evidence.'

'And that has the potential to complicate any investigation into him,' said Kennedy.

'I don't want to downplay things,' Jemima said, 'but as yet, we don't know if he poses a threat to anyone. It seems to me that I should have a word with Violet and find out from her what, if anything, has been going on.'

'Thank you, Sergeant. Once you've spoken with her, you'll realize that I'm not merely an overprotective grandfather. There is a real threat. I'll ring her now and make arrangements for you to meet.'

CHAPTER 4

Kennedy headed back to the police station, while Jemima set off in the opposite direction. The judge had been insistent that she speak to his granddaughter straight away, and arrangements had been made for her to meet Violet at a local coffee shop.

The streets were full of people making the most of their lunch break, and the unusually sunny weather had brought more people than usual out into the open. Jemima weaved her way through the lunchtime crowds. She couldn't help but think that this was going to be a complete waste of her time, but on the plus side, she wouldn't have to put up with Broadbent for the next hour or so.

The coffee shop was an independent enterprise, a rare treat with the increasing popularity of the big chains. It appeared to be a popular venue with the lunchtime crowd, as there was only one empty table. As Jemima scanned the seating area, she spotted Violet about two-thirds of the way across the room. She could tell that the young woman was nervous, as her arms were crossed so tightly across her chest that it gave the appearance she was hugging herself.

'Violet?' asked Jemima, as she approached the table.

Violet looked up, gave a weak smile and said hello.

'Is this for me?' asked Jemima, taking a seat opposite Violet.

'Yes, I hope you don't mind. I got you a latte. I thought it would save time. You're not allowed to sit here without ordering something.'

Jemima's initial assessment of Violet was that the young woman was serious and stressed. She wore a corporate black suit with a pale blouse buttoned to the bottom of her throat. Her hair was styled in a shoulder-length bob, which was both glossy and neat.

'Before we start, I have to ask if Lucy Goodman is a friend of yours?'

'Uh, yes,' Violet replied, tilting her head quizzically. 'How did you know that?'

'She's my sister. When your grandfather showed me a photograph of you, I thought you looked familiar.'

'Lucy's calling around to my house tomorrow,' said Violet. 'We've been planning a catch up for a while, but life always seems to get in the way. This is such an amazing coincidence.'

'Fill me in on what's been happening,' said Jemima, as she took out her notebook. Now that her question had been answered, she was determined to move things to a professional footing. She certainly didn't want to give Violet the impression that any relationship with her sister implied that Jemima and Violet would become friends.

'I moved to Cardiff about four months ago to take up a position at an NGO,' Violet began. 'Until that point in time, I had no intention of returning to Wales, but the post they offered me was too good an opportunity to turn down. I don't mean that it's lucrative, far from it. The attraction is that it's an exceptionally challenging role aimed at redressing inequalities in some of the world's poorest countries.

'When they heard that I was moving to Cardiff, my grandparents suggested that I live with them, which as far as I was concerned was a non-starter. I'm not able to buy a property at the moment, so I rented a house. It's a twelve-month contract, which allows me to put money aside for a deposit. It seemed like an ideal solution, but things started to go sour pretty quickly.

'A friend of my grandfather's owns a removal company, which came in handy as he brought some of my grandparents' furniture to this house completely free of charge. It wasn't much, just a bed, an old sofa and some chairs they were planning to get rid of. My grandparents were attending a social event in Surrey that weekend. They felt guilty about the timing, but I told them it didn't matter. It wasn't as if I needed their help. I was only taking my clothes and a few personal belongings, all of which I could easily fit into my car.

'I picked up the keys from the letting agent and drove to the property. The removal van was already there, so I parked outside my neighbour's house. As I got out of the car, I spotted him watching me from his lounge window. He smiled, so I smiled back. I only did it because I didn't want to start off on the wrong foot with any of the neighbours. But it turned out to be a huge mistake.'

'That was Byron Toombes? Why was it a mistake?' asked Jemima.

'Yes, it's Byron, and he immediately went from being someone I hadn't met to the creep I couldn't get rid of. And believe me, I've tried. You'll probably think I'm overreacting. It's not as if he's done anything to hurt me, but he's always there. He's either lurking in the background, or in my face trying to get me to go out with him. He doesn't take no for an answer, and it scares the hell out of me. He even gatecrashed a work event I held at my place. I'm scared of the fact that he doesn't respect boundaries and doesn't acknowledge that he's acting unacceptably.'

'I'll need a list of everyone who attended that event in case I need to speak to them.'

'Do you have to?'

'If he leaves you alone from now on, then no, I won't have to. But if his harassment of you continues, then yes, I'll need to speak to them. There's also a possibility that he could ramp things up. If things head in that direction, it'll be important to gather as much independent evidence against him as possible. Did you challenge him when he gatecrashed your event?'

'No. I felt embarrassed. We'd already wrapped up the work element and had moved on to the social side of things. There was music playing and lots of chatter. I didn't hear the doorbell as I was in the kitchen. When I returned to the lounge, I found Byron there socializing with some of my colleagues. I was shocked and angry, but I didn't want to make a scene and spoil the evening. I was worried about what they'd think if I told him to leave.'

'I appreciate that he put you in an awkward situation, but was there more to it than you're saying?' asked Jemima.

'Yes, Byron disappeared at one stage, and I thought he'd gone home. I felt so relieved. I headed upstairs to get something from my bedroom and walked in to find him and one of my colleagues having sex on my bed! I couldn't believe it. It was so inappropriate. I still feel sick at the thought of it.'

'What did you do?' asked Jemima.

'It wasn't my finest moment. I completely lost it. I told Byron that I never wanted to speak to him again and ordered them both to leave. He left me in peace for a few days after that, but he's started to pester me again. It's got to the stage where I'm afraid to set foot outside the house. But I've got to go to work and do normal everyday things. My life's a living nightmare. I spend most of my time looking over my sho— Oh no!'

'What's the matter?' asked Jemima. As she looked across at Violet, she noticed the colour drain from the woman's cheeks.

'It's him — Toombes. He's just walked in. He keeps doing this. He follows me all the time. You've got to make him stop. Please, you have to help me,' begged Violet. She was visibly trembling, and her voice crackled with fear. 'He's coming over. What should I do?'

'Speak loudly and firmly so that everyone can hear what you're saying. Tell Toombes that you don't want to have any contact with him and that he has to stop following you,' said Jemima. She barely had time to finish the sentence before Toombes arrived at their table.

'Well, what a surprise! It must be fate pushing us together. I'm glad I bumped into you, Violet. I've got a couple of tickets for the New Theatre tomorrow evening. Perhaps you'd like to go with me?'

Toombes was standing side-on to their table, and his focus was entirely upon Violet. It allowed Jemima the opportunity to get a good look at him, without his noticing that she was studying him. There was nothing exceptional about his appearance. His body language appeared relaxed and non-threatening. He had a pleasant face, and was of average height and build with dark hair. To any casual observer, there was nothing about him that would cause anyone to become immediately wary. He was mister average.

Violet took a deep breath before she spoke. 'No, I don't want to go anywhere with you. I've given you no reason to think that I want anything to do with you, so stop following me and leave me alone.'

As Violet rebuffed Byron Toombes, Jemima watched the man's stance stiffen and the smile fade on his lips. She also noticed a vein become more pronounced on his temple and his hands bunch into fists, though, when he next spoke, his voice was light and unconcerned.

'I'm not following you, Violet. How could you even think that? I was going to call round this evening to invite you to the theatre, but as I was walking past I glanced through the window and saw you, so I thought that I may as well ask you now. It was just me being impulsive, nothing more.'

'Let me be clear. I don't want to have anything to do with you,' said Violet, emboldened by the fact that Jemima was with her. 'Just because I have the misfortune of living next door to you, it doesn't mean that we are, or ever will be, friends. So stop calling around to my house, stop following me, and don't ever speak to me again.'

'There's no need—' began Toombes.

'Mr Toombes, I suggest you walk away. Violet has already told you that she wants nothing to do with you,' began Jemima.

'And who the hell are you?' asked Toombes.

'I'm a police officer, Mr Toombes, and you are harassing this woman. Now I suggest you walk away, and in future keep your distance from her, unless you want a restraining order issued against you.'

'B-but—' stuttered Toombes.

'But nothing, Mr Toombes. Take my advice and walk away. It's clear to me, and every other person in this room, that Miss Watkins wants to have no contact with you, so listen to what she's told you and leave her alone.'

'Fine,' muttered Toombes. The vein on his temple was even more pronounced, and there was a malicious glint in his eye.

CHAPTER 5

Jemima escorted Violet back to her place of work. It wasn't something she would normally consider doing, but it was obvious that Violet was in no fit state to be on her own. Her fragility was evident. A passing car had backfired, and Violet had jumped and squealed in terror. The young woman was noticeably shaken by the encounter with Toombes. She explained to Jemima that she was afraid of walking alone, even though it was the middle of the day. As they parted company, it was agreed that Jemima would call round to Violet's house at five o'clock that evening to take a formal statement from her.

Back at the station, Jemima headed towards her desk. Broadbent looked up and smiled maliciously as he spotted Kennedy walking towards her.

'You've just had a long lunch break, Sarge,' said Broadbent. His voice was loud, and there was no mistaking his intent. It was a blatant attempt at seizing the opportunity to get Jemima into trouble. 'Sorry, sir, I didn't see you there. Anything I can do to help?' he asked Kennedy innocently.

Jemima and Kennedy both knew what he was up to and exchanged a furtive glance.

'No thank you, Broadbent. Huxley, my office,' said Kennedy.

Jemima dropped her belongings on the desk and followed Kennedy.

'What's your impression of Violet Watkins?' he asked, but only after they had reached his office and he had shut the door.

'I think she's genuinely scared of Toombes. It seems as though he fixated on her as soon as she moved in next door. We didn't have much chance to talk, as he walked into the coffee shop as bold as brass and offered to take her out on a date.'

'While you were with her?' asked Kennedy, his eyebrows arching in disbelief.

'Yeah — it was as though there was no one else around. Violet told him where to go and said she wanted nothing to do with him. But he wasn't getting the message. I'm convinced he's playing mind games with her. Gaslighting her to erode her confidence and make her appear paranoid. He's also clever. To anyone who doesn't know what he's up to, he'd come across as a reasonable guy. Certainly not menacing. But I think there's a possibility he might be dangerous.'

'What do you base that assessment on?' asked Kennedy.

'Just little things. He's quite skilled at hiding his intentions, but not skilled enough. His body language suggests he's got a temper. Though he's controlled enough to hide it. I ended up having to tell him to back off, and he didn't appreciate the interference. It was only when I identified myself as a police officer that he slinked away.'

'So what's your next move?' asked Kennedy.

'I'm going to Violet's house at five o'clock. I'll take an official statement and advise her of ways to stay safe. For the next hour or so, I thought I'd do some digging around on Byron Toombes. See what I can find out. As he's a SOCO, he won't have a criminal record. But that doesn't mean he hasn't pushed his luck before now, and I'd be surprised if Violet is the first woman he's fixated on.'

'Good idea. While you're doing that, I'll do my best to keep soft lad out of your hair. We may very well have to bring him in on this at a later stage, but for now, we keep the circle small. When you return to your desk, tell him I want to see him. That should wipe the smug smile off his face.'

Jemima delivered Kennedy's message to Broadbent, and as soon as Broadbent left the room, she got to work. As SOCOs were employed by police forces, her first port of call was to the person in charge of that unit, in this case a woman called Yvette De Sousa. She phoned ahead to make an appointment with Yvette, explaining that this was an urgent matter but refusing to give any details over the telephone.

It was the first time the two women had come face to face, and Jemima was surprised both by Yvette's physical appearance and by her eagerness to help. As often happens, the image of Yvette that Jemima had conjured up in her head turned out to be completely at odds with the actual person. For some reason, Jemima had expected to find a mousey-haired middle-aged woman with poor dress sense. Instead, the woman standing before her was striking. At six foot tall, with short, spiky red hair and cheekbones to die for, Yvette De Sousa would stand out in any crowd. And if anything, she was even younger than Jemima.

'So, how can I be of help?' asked Yvette.

'I'm investigating a complaint about one of the SOCOs. I've only just been made aware of the allegations, but they are very serious. Apart from my inspector, you will be the third person to be made aware of his identity. And due to the nature of the complaint, I would ask for your complete discretion.'

'That goes without saying,' reassured Yvette. 'Who is the employee in question?'

'His name's Byron Toombes.'

'Ooh,' said Yvette. Her pronunciation of the word was noticeably protracted.

'I take it that you know him?' asked Jemima.

'Oh, yes, I know him. What's he done?'

'I'm afraid I can't divulge that information. But I would be interested in getting your take on him.'

25

'My "take" on Byron Toombes is that he's a danger to women. He's a rapist, but nothing's ever going to be done about it.' The statement was delivered with anger, and there was no attempt to hide the contempt Yvette so obviously felt towards the man.

Jemima hadn't expected to hear anything like that but had no doubt that Yvette meant every word she said. As well as the marked change in her voice, the woman's expression had darkened. And Jemima thought she saw the glint of tears in the young woman's eyes.

'Tell me everything you know,' encouraged Jemima.

'That animal raped my sister. But given the circumstances in which the rape occurred, my sister felt unable to report it.'

'Why?' asked Jemima.

'My sister was a student at the time. And just like every other student, she needed to have a regular income. Instead of going down a traditional route earning a pittance in a bar or a shop, Stella decided to sign up with an escort agency. She kept it from everyone in our family. You see, we grew up in a very conservative household. Our father would have a heart attack if he ever found out about it. Toombes was one of Stella's clients. I don't know the precise details of what he did, but I know that it culminated in rape. Is that what he's accused of now?'

'I've already told you that I can't go into specifics, but I'd be very interested in speaking with your sister. Read into that what you will.'

Yvette sat forward in her chair, narrowed her eyes, and stared at Jemima as she silently appraised her. The level of scrutiny was slightly disconcerting, and Jemima was about to break the silence when the woman sat back and spoke.

'You may also want to speak to a woman named Catrin Pembry. She was a SOCO based at Cardiff. She transferred to the Gwent force about a year ago — this was well before Toombes started seeing my sister. Catrin didn't officially reveal why she requested a transfer, but I understand that she worked on the same team as Toombes. And I've heard from more than one source that there were rumours he may have been the reason she felt unable to continue working here.

'I have a feeling that Stella can trust you, so I'll give her a call and ask her to talk to you this evening. I'm sure she wouldn't want anyone else to experience what Toombes put her through. After the rape, my sister moved in with me. So you can talk to her at my place. Hopefully, she'll feel reassured as I'll be there too. She's been evasive whenever I've broached the subject with her, but perhaps she'll open up to you.'

'I'll call round at about seven o'clock,' said Jemima, making a note of Yvette's address.

CHAPTER 6

Jemima returned to her desk, picked up the phone and dialled the number Yvette De Sousa had texted her. When Jemima introduced herself, Catrin Pembry sounded curious, but as soon as Byron Toombes's name was mentioned, the woman's voice hardened, and she insisted that she was too busy to talk.

Not being the sort of person to be easily put off, Jemima decided to play hardball. 'I'm not going to go away, Catrin. If you don't talk to me now, I'll turn up at your workplace and speak to you there. It's up to you. We can either do this quietly over the telephone or risk having your colleagues find out about it.'

'Fine,' hissed Catrin, accepting that Jemima meant what she said. 'As long as you understand that what happened to me is in the past. I'll give you the facts, but I've no intention of making a complaint against him. If you want to know what happened, you'll have to meet me, as it's not the sort of thing I want to talk about over the phone.'

* * *

Forty minutes later, Jemima walked into a pub on the out-skirts of Newport. As she scanned the room, she spotted a lone female nursing a glass. After ordering a drink from the bar, Jemima took a seat opposite Catrin.

'Was Byron Toombes the reason you transferred to another police force?' asked Jemima.

'Absolutely, he's not right in the head. We were colleagues, nothing more, but for some reason, he didn't see it that way. I've always been clear about my sexuality. I'm in a lesbian relationship and have no interest in men whatsoever, but Toombes had other ideas. It was a war of attrition. He was clever enough not to do anything when others were around, but whenever it was just the two of us, it was a different matter. It got to the stage where I didn't feel safe at work or in my own home.'

'He pestered you outside of work too?'

'Yeah, he did. He's a sex pest all right. It reached the stage where I felt as though I didn't have a safe space. It was exhausting and debilitating. I couldn't live like that.'

'Why didn't you report him?' asked Jemima, though she was sure that she already knew the reason why.

'In an ideal world, I would have. But I couldn't. You know the misogynistic arseholes we have to put up with. Do you honestly think that I would have been treated fairly if I'd brought a case of sexual harassment against Toombes?'

'Fair point,' said Jemima.

It was one thing having laws in place to protect people, but those laws were far from adequate. If Catrin had pursued a case against Toombes, there was a small chance that they would have found him guilty, but as a victim, Catrin would have had to continue working alongside colleagues who would consider her to be a troublemaker. From then on, she ran the risk of being targeted in an insidious campaign to undermine her confidence and credibility. Certain colleagues would make her life increasingly difficult until she felt there was no option available to her other than to resign.

'Exactly. If I'd spoken up, I wouldn't just have been the lesbian they could snigger at when my back was turned. I'd be the ruthless man-hating bitch who was on a mission to destroy every man's career. No one would want to work with me, and I'd have flushed my career prospects away for nothing. I love my job, and I'm bloody good at it. I wasn't going to let that piece of shit take it away from me.'

'What exactly did Toombes do to you?'

'Nothing much at first, just the odd glance and inappropriately suggestive comment. Nothing I haven't heard before. Then there was one particularly busy day when we were short-staffed. I was unlucky enough to draw the short straw and had to partner up with Toombes. There was just the two of us in the vehicle when he told me that he'd dreamed about me and couldn't stop thinking about it. I told him to shut up, that I wasn't interested, but he just kept on talking. He came out with a load of filth, about things he had done to me, and when I glanced down, I noticed that he was hard. I felt sick. But we were on the motorway, and there was nowhere for me to go. I was stuck inside the vehicle with him — trapped. That's when he touched me and told me that he knew I wanted it too.'

'That's awful,' said Jemima.

'That wasn't the worst of it. I reached out to push his hand away, but Toombes was too quick for me and grabbed my hand. His grip was like a vice. As I struggled, he momentarily lost control of the steering wheel, and the van lurched sideways. It was a close call. We almost hit another vehicle. There were horns blaring and lights flashing. I thought we were going to die.

'I closed my eyes and screamed. When I opened them again, Toombes was grinning like an idiot. At first, I didn't realize why, but as my heart rate began to return to normal, I looked down. That's when I saw that he'd placed my hand on his groin. I don't know why I hadn't felt it until then — I suppose it must have been the near brush with death. When we reached our destination, I leaped out of the vehicle and threw up. Luckily, I didn't have to travel back with him, as I managed to blag a lift from a PC who was heading back to the station.

'It was after that incident that the anonymous phone calls started. Of course, they were untraceable, and I ended up having to change my mobile number. Then one evening, as I was leaving my house, I found him leaning up against my car. My partner Judy was away at the time, and somehow he knew that. He said it was the perfect opportunity for us to spend some quality time together.'

'So he was stalking you?' asked Jemima.

'Definitely, but there wasn't anything I could do about it. I feared for my safety. Nowhere was off-limits to Toombes. He saw me at work, and he knew where I lived. He'd obviously been watching the house because I hadn't told anyone that Judy had gone away for a while. It scared the hell out of me.

'I knew that there was no point in reporting it, as it would just be his word against mine. And if I went down that route, I could kiss my career goodbye. So I put in for a transfer. Luckily for me, a vacancy came up with the Gwent force. It was also fortunate that Judy and I were only renting the property we lived in. It was near the end of our contract. So we moved out of Cardiff, and I didn't give anyone our new address.'

'Drastic measures,' said Jemima.

'Drastic but necessary,' said Catrin. 'Byron Toombes has a screw loose. You can't deal with him the way you would with any reasonably well-adjusted person. And you certainly can't second-guess what he'll do if he becomes upset. I didn't want to end up raped or dead, so I did what I had to do, and it was a small price to pay.'

CHAPTER 7

Violet's house was located on a quiet side street. A sign at the entrance to the road indicated that it was a dead end, which gave the street the advantage of not being used as a rat run. As Jemima pulled up outside, she noted that the area appeared well kept. When she stepped out of the car, the only noticeable sound was the faint rumble of traffic along the nearby main road.

Jemima rang the doorbell. She noticed a slight movement of the Venetian blind that covered the downstairs window. It was a good sign, as it was apparent that Violet had the sense to check who was at the front door before opening it.

Once inside, Jemima's initial impression was that the house had a homely feel. The furniture, though old-fashioned, had been given a new lease of life with a variety of plump, bright cushions and throws. Modern prints hung on the walls. Everything looked clean and tidy, and scented candles perfumed the air.

'Come through to the kitchen. I was just about to make a cuppa,' said Violet.

Jemima hoisted herself on to a barstool and waited for Violet to prepare the drink before she went ahead with her fact-finding task. She placed her notebook and pen on the work surface to enable her to record any pertinent facts. 'Any further problems with him since we last spoke?' she asked, when Violet had taken the barstool opposite her.

'None whatsoever. I've not heard any sound from next door either, so he's probably still at work.'

'That's good. It was clear from what I witnessed at the coffee shop that Byron's determined to get your attention. Stalkers engineer ways to get you to interact with them. He'll want you to be thinking about him as much as he's thinking about you.'

'You think he's stalking me?'

'It's highly likely, and I believe you should think of him in that way. Give me a detailed account of every encounter you've had with him since you first met and consider his likely motivation behind those interactions. I also want you to think about things that you've done and the effect they may have had on his behaviour.'

'I haven't encouraged him.'

'I'm not judging you, Violet. I just need you to realize that from now on you have to modify your behaviour, and quite possibly change the way you live your life. It's unfair, but it's for your own safety. You have to put yourself in Byron's shoes and think about what he's likely to do and how he's likely to react.' Jemima turned to an empty page of her notebook and picked up her pen.

'I've already told you that when I first arrived, Byron was watching me from inside his house. He obviously saw that I was all on my own. He smiled at me, and I was foolish enough to smile back.'

'Why did you smile at him?' asked Jemima.

'It was just a friendly gesture, nothing more than that, but I guess he saw it as a sign that I was up for some sort of a relationship with him,' said Violet.

'That could very well be an accurate assessment. I may stop you as you tell me more, just to get you to think about things in a new light, but continue for now,' said Jemima.

'After the removal men went, hardly any time had passed when there was a knock on the door. When I opened

33

the door, Byron was standing there with a massive bouquet of flowers and an expensive box of chocolates. To be honest, it immediately made me feel uncomfortable, as the gesture was way over the top. In retrospect, I think he played me right from the start. Knowing what I now know about him, I realize that I should have told him to back off.'

'I think you're right. Those gifts are the sort of thing you'd give to someone when you're trying to impress them on a first date.'

'Exactly, it made me feel awkward, but I was brought up in a household where social niceties were observed. It was drummed into me that it was important to do the right thing, to be polite and respectful.'

'I'm sure I don't need to tell you that we all make assumptions about people based on non-verbal cues,' Jemima told her. 'Things such as the way you dress, the car you drive, the way you speak, your general demeanour.'

'So when he looked out of the window, in those first few seconds, he would have picked up on the fact that I dress in a conformist way, and my smile told him that I was friendly?'

'I think you're getting the hang of this,' said Jemima, smiling encouragingly. 'You became a target the moment he set eyes upon you and liked what he saw. Everything about you screams conventionality, which is a weakness when you're pitted against a predator. That was his way in. He read you like a book and had a high degree of certainty about how you'd react. It allowed him to call the shots. I take it that you felt obliged to let him in?'

'Yes, and that was a big mistake,' said Violet.

'What happened?'

'He must have noticed that I was conflicted. I didn't feel comfortable about allowing a complete stranger into the house, and I definitely felt awkward about accepting the gifts. But I also knew that if I told him to go away, we would start off on the wrong foot. My parents always said that good neighbours are like gold dust. And apart from the over-the-top gesture, he was perfectly polite, albeit a bit pushy.

'I thought I could get him to take the flowers back by telling him that I didn't have a vase. But he told me it wasn't a problem and got one of his own. When I told him that I was busy unpacking, he got stuck in and helped. It was embarrassing, but he wouldn't take no for an answer. He said it was important to be a good neighbour and show kindness to those in need. And in fairness, he was a great help. That's why I let my guard down and asked him over for takeout that evening. I thought it would make us quits.'

'But it didn't?' said Jemima.

'No, the evening started off OK. Byron brought a bottle of wine, so I felt obliged to open it. I rarely drink alcohol but thought it'd be churlish not to have a glass. We sat on these bar stools and ate the food. He asked why no one had helped me with the move. I stupidly told him the truth, so he realized that I was isolated.

'He told me that he'd just come out of a relationship with someone named Stella. He said that it had happened when he was particularly vulnerable, as both his parents had recently died in a traffic collision. I put a hand on his arm. It was a supportive gesture, as I felt sorry for him. It encouraged him to open up even more, and he told me that he was suffering from depression. He began to cry and said he couldn't face eating more of the food. He asked if we could sit in the lounge. There were still boxes and piles of things littering the place. The only free seat was the two-seater sofa, which meant that we ended up sitting far too close to each other.'

'How did that make you feel?' asked Jemima.

'Uneasy. I didn't want to be that close to him, but I didn't feel able to dump the things off one of the other chairs as he'd just been telling me how he felt so alone and had suicidal thoughts. In hindsight, I realize that he was forcing me to react the way he wanted me to. He was trying to ensure that I felt obliged to interact with him. He knew that I wouldn't want to feel responsible for pushing him over the edge. I stupidly even told him that he could talk to me whenever he needed a shoulder to cry on.'

'So, in other words, he sucked you in. Byron got you to believe that if you rejected him, you would be responsible for any future suicide attempt?'

'Yes, I guess that he guilt-tripped me.'

'Exactly. In the space of a few hours, he had you dancing to his tune.'

'You're very good at reading behaviour,' said Violet.

'It's a skill I have to use every day. It also helps that I have a degree in psychology. But this is something you'll have to learn for yourself. When I'm gone, I want you to write down everything you've said, along with every other interaction you've had with him. Include dates, times, locations, and the names of anyone who has witnessed these events. If he persists in his pursuit of you, you'll be able to take out a restraining order against him. But with any luck, he may just decide that you're not worth the hassle. After all, he already knows that you've contacted the police. If things continue to escalate, he runs the risk of losing his job. Make sure that the house is always locked up securely, even when you're inside. Don't open the door to anyone unless you know who's there.'

CHAPTER 8

Despite not being far away, it took almost forty minutes for Jemima to reach her next destination. After locking the car, she approached the house, rang the doorbell and waited. Moments later the door was opened by Yvette De Sousa. There was no evidence of the corporate persona. She was dressed in lime-green jeggings and a yellow T-shirt. The striking combination looked good on her and emphasized her svelte form. And Jemima marvelled at the fact that the woman somehow exuded energy and positivity.

'Come in,' said Yvette. 'Stella's waiting for you in the lounge, though she's not happy about having to talk to you.'

Stella De Sousa was even more attractive than her sister, and Jemima could immediately understand why she would have been a popular choice of escort. She was slightly shorter than Yvette, though still taller than average, with lustrous chestnut-brown hair that flowed over her shoulders in natural waves. With facial features softer than Yvette's, her large brown eyes and full lips gave her the look of someone who could easily grace the cover of any glossy magazine.

It was immediately apparent to Jemima that Stella was uncomfortable in her presence. And as soon as she spoke, the reason became clear.

'Apart from my sister, you're the only other person who knows what Byron did to me,' said Stella. 'I was horrified when Yvette told me that she wanted me to speak to you. I'd sworn her to secrecy. I didn't want anyone to know what had happened to me, or what I did to make ends meet.'

'I'm not here to judge you, Stella. Just to find out what happened, as it may have a bearing on a current investigation. I'm interested in anything you can tell me about Toombes.'

'Has he done it to someone else?' Stella asked. The mere thought of it caused her eyes to fill with tears.

Jemima noticed that Stella was unable to use the word 'rape', as she was undoubtedly trying to distance herself from what Toombes had done to her.

'If you're asking whether I'm investigating a rape, then the answer is no. But I am worried about Byron Toombes's behaviour towards a young woman who is about the same age as you. I believe he could be a threat to her, and I'm currently trying to ascertain the level of danger she could be in. Anything you're able to tell me could potentially help me understand what makes him tick. At the moment I really don't know what I'm dealing with.'

'OK, if you think it'll help. I don't want that pervert to hurt anyone else.' Stella shuddered as she took a deep breath, then folded her arms tightly across her chest. 'I met Byron when I was an escort. I'd signed up with Select Escort Services. It was only ever meant to be a short-term fix to see me through university. In retrospect, I wish I hadn't gone down that route. But everything's so expensive, and I was finding it difficult to make ends meet.

'I was studying for a law degree. It's very intense. There's so much to learn, so I needed to find a well-paid, part-time job that I could fit around my studies. Believe it or not, there aren't many options — especially ones that offer flexible working hours. It seemed that every employer was offering the minimum wage. And I knew that I wouldn't be able to commit to working enough hours to make a sufficient amount of money.

'Someone on my course suggested that I should consider signing up with the agency as they have quite a few students on their books. My initial reaction was to steer clear, but the more I thought about it, the more it seemed the ideal solution.'

'When you signed up with them, was it in the expectation that you would have sex with the clients?' asked Jemima.

'No. The agency was clear from the outset that they weren't pimping escorts out, though they knew that many of us agreed to off-the-book optional extras. Their business model is targeted at wealthy individuals. Often they're lonely businesspeople visiting the city for a few days for work purposes. Despite the agency's exorbitant hourly rates, there's no shortage of people prepared to part with such ridiculous amounts of money. It enables them to spend a few hours in the company of another human being.

'Most of the time, I just had dinner or drinks with someone, with the occasional theatre trip thrown in. The hardest thing was being a plus-one at corporate social events. I treated it as though it was an acting role. I'd have to quickly familiarize myself with the facts the client had shared with me. It was always important to them that no one knew they had paid for my company. It's quite a challenging thing to do. You have to ensure your interaction with the client appears natural so that others believe you're in an actual relationship. Those assignments were hard work but enjoyable. I often got tipped really well at the end of the evening.

'On some occasions, I was booked to spend the evening with lonely female executives desperate for the company of another woman. They'd spend the time chatting about ordinary things in a non-threatening scenario. I suppose it was more appealing to them than booking a table for one at a hotel restaurant. The truth is that I had sex with very few of the clients, and that's the way I liked it.'

'So how did Byron end up on the agency's books? After all, he's not some wealthy businessman in town for a few days. He doesn't have a high salary and he lives locally. As far as I can tell, he doesn't fit any of the client profiles you've just described.'

'I agree. Toombes was an odd one. You say he didn't have a high salary, but he was never short of money. He was always splashing the cash. At first, I was reluctant to take him on as a regular, but he offered me a hell of a lot extra if I kept seeing him and agreed to a particular request of his. It was a regular cash transaction just between the two of us.'

'Did you regularly have sex with Byron?' asked Jemima.

'No. The only occasion was when he raped me.'

'What was his request?'

'I don't feel comfortable talking about that in front of my sister,' said Stella. She lowered her head in an attempt to hide the fact that her cheeks had reddened with embarrassment.

'Seriously?' said Yvette. 'I thought we didn't have secrets anymore?'

'Could you give us some time alone?' asked Jemima. The last thing she needed was for the sisters to fall out and Stella to clam up altogether.

'Fine,' said Yvette, as she marched out of the room in a manner that left them both in no doubt that she was unhappy about being asked to leave.

'Shall I shut the door?' asked Jemima.

Stella nodded.

'I'm sorry to keep pushing you, but what did Byron ask you to do?' Jemima asked as she sat back down.

'He's a voyeur. He set up a webcam in my bedroom and liked to watch me doing things to myself. I told him that I wasn't happy about it. I was concerned that he'd record it then post it on the internet for others to see. He insisted that he wouldn't and assured me it would be just for him. He even gave me a face mask to hide my identity. He didn't force me into it. He said he'd give me some time to think about it, and that it would be entirely my decision. And when I thought about it, I came to realize that it could be anyone behind the mask. It wasn't as if anyone would know it was me. He also paid me a hundred pounds a time. It was a no-brainer.'

'What happened to cause him to transition from voyeur to rapist?'

'It was a completely different set of circumstances. It was the weekend of the Brecon Jazz Festival, and he booked me for the entire weekend. He'd bought tickets for us to see six different acts.'

'That must have cost him a fortune,' said Jemima.

'It did, and he gave me five hundred cash in addition to that. When I agreed to accompany him, I thought we'd be staying at a hotel. But we weren't. What I didn't realize was that he had a property close to Brecon. He called it his country retreat. It was a remote, old-fashioned cottage, which he said he'd recently acquired from an elderly couple. I wasn't particularly happy, but I couldn't do anything about it. I kept telling myself that everything would be fine, and it was. If it hadn't been for that final morning, I would have had a great time.'

'Are you able to tell me what happened?' asked Jemima.

'It was a Monday morning. We'd slept in separate bedrooms since we'd arrived. It was early. I heard him moving about in the other room and thought he was going to go downstairs, but instead, he came into my bedroom. I saw something in his hand but couldn't quite make out what it was. The next thing I knew, he was straddling me, and I realized that he had a set of handcuffs. I screamed and struggled. He punched the side of my head. I must have passed out because the next thing I knew, he was inside me and my wrists were cuffed to the bed frame. There was nothing I could do.

'When it was all over, he apologized as if it made everything all right. When he uncuffed me, he placed another hundred on the bedside cabinet. He told me to shower and get changed as we had a funeral to attend.'

'A funeral?' Jemima thought she must have misheard what Stella had just said.

'Yes. Byron's parents were killed when a lorry collided with their car. Not that I had any idea until he told me. He certainly wasn't upset about their deaths. In fact, it was their house that we were staying in. I'd been sleeping in their bed.

'I just wanted to get away from him, so I did as I was told. We attended their funeral service. Then he drove me home as though nothing had happened. I realized that morning that he was completely unhinged. I was terrified. When we arrived back in Cardiff, he took my case out of the car, kissed me on the cheek and said that he'd see me in a few days. It was as though he hadn't attacked me and that everything was perfectly normal.

'I rang the agency straightaway, told them what had happened and quit. Becoming an escort was the biggest mistake of my life. It's something I'd prefer to forget.'

CHAPTER 9

The following morning, as Jemima was taking her coat off, she was summoned to Kennedy's office.

'How did yesterday's fact-finding mission go?' he asked.

'I'm convinced Toombes is a sexual predator. He's targeted two women and raped a third. Catrin and Stella gave credible accounts of their experiences. He's got no boundaries and doesn't take no for an answer. There's no doubt in my mind that he's a danger to Violet.'

'It's not looking good,' said Kennedy, sighing deeply as he shook his head in despair. 'Not only have we got ourselves a sex offender, but he just happens to be someone who knows about forensics and has had ample opportunity to tamper with evidence from God knows how many crime scenes. Do we have enough evidence to question him?'

'No. Stella De Sousa is adamant that she won't testify, and I don't blame her. She didn't report it at the time, and there's no chance of getting any physical evidence to back up her claims. Catrin Pembry also has no intention of taking things forward — not that there would have been any physical evidence to build a case against him. It would have just been a case of "he said, she said".'

'In other words we have to watch and wait, unless Toombes makes a move on Violet,' said Kennedy. 'In which case we have to hope we can react in time.'

'I'm not comfortable with the idea of treating her as bait,' said Jemima.

'Neither am I, but I can't see we can do much else at the moment, apart from beefing up her home security and ensuring she's got a personal safety alarm.'

'I was thinking about carrying out some background checks on Toombes and seeing what that throws up,' said Jemima.

'Good idea. I also think it's time to bring soft lad in on things. I know he's acted like a prat since you've arrived, but he's a decent copper. If Broadbent can overcome his resentment towards you, I think the pair of you could make a decent team. He just needs to put that bruised ego of his back in the box.

'With regard to Toombes, it's entirely conceivable that things may escalate pretty quickly. It'll be too much for you to handle by yourself, and Broadbent's a good officer to have on side. I'll tell him to come in and the three of us can talk things through. I'll make sure there'll be no doubt in his mind that he's got to change his ways. I guarantee he'll see things differently in a few moments.'

Broadbent's delight at being summoned by Kennedy was clear to see, as he all but bounced into the room, though the smile quickly faded on his lips the moment he realized that Jemima was already there. His thought process was all too transparent and wasn't lost on Kennedy.

'Park yourself down, lad. We've things to discuss,' said Kennedy, sitting back in his seat. He folded his arms and stretched out his legs.

'Before you get started, you need to realize that it was just a bit of banter,' said Broadbent. He was doing his best to keep his voice light and his body language open, but it was evident to both of them that he thought he'd been summoned because Jemima had complained about him.

'I haven't a clue what you're on about, lad, and quite frankly I don't want to know. I've asked you here to bring you up to speed on a case that Huxley and I have been made aware of. I didn't bring you in on it right at the start because for the last few weeks you've been acting like an idiot and it has to stop.'

'What have you been telling him?' asked Broadbent as he turned to glare at Jemima.

'She hasn't told me anything, lad. Huxley's far too professional for that. Now, you've worked with me for long enough to know that I'm a damn good copper. Nothing gets past me — and that includes the way you've been making her life hell. It's time you had a wake-up call, Broadbent — and this is it. The harsh reality is that you didn't get the sergeant's post because you weren't up to it. And Huxley didn't get it because there was some quota we needed to meet so as not to fall foul of the equal opportunity law. The only reason she got the job is because she was the best person for it — end of!

'Now, I suggest that you stop acting like a spoilt brat, knuckle down, and prove to us that you're a team player. You need to accept that you've got an excellent sergeant. And as far as I'm concerned, she's not going anywhere. You can learn a lot from her, and who knows, further down the line you may actually deserve a sergeant's post. But think on — blot your copybook further and those stains will remain there for the rest of your career. If that happens, you'll consider yourself lucky being allowed to direct traffic. Are we clear, lad?'

As Jemima glanced across, she knew that the words had hit home. Broadbent clearly hadn't expected Kennedy to lay it on the line so forcefully. He was wide-eyed, shell-shocked and deflated. His shoulders slumped under the weight of what had just been said, and his mouth hung open as he attempted to formulate an acceptable response. All in all, he looked as though he'd been slapped across the face with a wet kipper.

'I'm expecting an answer, Broadbent,' pressed Kennedy.

'Uh?' said Broadbent as he looked up.

45

'Are you prepared to settle down and make the best of things? Because if the answer's no, I've got a transfer request form ready for you to fill in.' Kennedy slid open the top drawer of his pedestal, extracted the document and pushed it towards Broadbent.

Even Jemima was surprised at the steely edge to Kennedy's voice.

'I-I'm sorry if I took things too far. Y-you won't have any more trouble from me,' muttered Broadbent. He swallowed hastily, unable to look directly at either of them.

'Apology accepted,' said Jemima, and she meant it. Broadbent had been a thorn in her side, but Kennedy appeared to be a good judge of character, and he was obviously prepared to give Broadbent the benefit of the doubt. After the humiliating dressing down he'd just endured, she actually felt sorry for Broadbent.

'See lad, it's so much better when we all act like adults,' said Kennedy. 'But I'll be keeping an eye on you.'

As they walked back towards their desks, Jemima noticed that Broadbent was trembling. There were beads of sweat on his forehead, and his skin had taken on a slightly greyish hue.

'Let's grab a coffee,' she said, as she placed a hand on his shoulder and steered him towards the canteen.

Broadbent did as he was told, and when Jemima suggested he should take a seat at one of the many empty tables, he didn't object. She headed towards the counter and returned a few minutes later, carrying a tray with two steaming mugs of coffee and a couple of sticky buns. The sharp reprimand was clearly still affecting Broadbent, as his elbows were on the table and his forehead rested heavily on his palms.

'Thought you could do with a sugar rush,' said Jemima, as she pushed the cake towards him.

'Thanks, that's really generous of you. It's my favourite,' Broadbent said with a weak smile.

'I know, that's why I got it. I've seen you eat one most days.'

'I really don't deserve it — not after the way I've treated you.'

'That's in the past. It's a new start, and I'm determined to make our partnership work. So here's to us,' said Jemima as she raised her mug and held it out as a toast.

'Yeah, to us,' Broadbent responded. 'I am genuinely sorry for the way I've treated you. It was wrong and stupid, but I let some of the guys get to me. It was hard not to when they kept dripping poison in my ear. It's important you know that I'm not a sexist prick. It was jealousy because I wanted the promotion. But you can trust me. I'm a team player.'

It was the most he'd said to her since Jemima had taken up the sergeant's post, but Jemima wasn't naive enough to believe that Broadbent would have her back from now on. It was one thing to accept that you had to change your behaviour, but that was quite different from changing your mindset, as often prejudices were set in stone.

Jemima knew that the wise course of action would be to continue to be wary of Broadbent. His animosity towards her wouldn't have magically disappeared. If anything, it would become more covert. To elicit a genuine change in his behaviour, she needed to gain his trust. And in order to do that, she needed to demonstrate that she wasn't one to hold a grudge.

'As far as I'm concerned, the slate's been wiped clean and we should move on. We've more important things to worry about at the moment. Have you ever worked on a stalking case before?' asked Jemima.

'No, have you?'

'Unfortunately not, so we're both going to have to get up to speed pretty quickly. I'd like you to dig into Toombes's background. From what I've heard, he's got money — far more than he earns from being a SOCO. See what you can find out about that.'

'I've come across him at crime scenes. Not spoken to him though.'

'What was your take on him?'

'He didn't seem to gel with the others. You know what it's like — you pick up on banter, read body language. It's things we do without thinking, a sort of sixth sense. When you see the same faces at work situations, you sort of know who gets on with whom. But Toombes always seems aloof.'

'That's interesting,' said Jemima. 'We can't afford to tip our hand too early, but when the time is right, it'd be sensible to interview his work colleagues. In the meantime, I'm going to give myself a crash course on best practice for dealing with a stalker.'

* * *

When they returned to their desks, the first task for Jemima was to reacquaint herself with the DASH Risk Identification and Assessment Model, which gave a framework for professionals working in areas of public protection to follow in various scenarios, including stalking and harassment. Following the methodology would allow her to undertake a risk analysis. It was a twenty-seven-item checklist that she would need to complete. Questions eight and fifteen related specifically to stalking and harassment, which in turn led to an additional eleven questions being asked.

Time passed quickly, as Jemima and Broadbent were both engrossed in their respective tasks. When her phone rang, Jemima jumped. She could tell straight away that it was her sister and was shocked to hear Lucy shouting. As Jemima's mind raced, she recalled Violet telling her that Lucy would be spending time with her that evening.

In the background, Jemima could hear muffled shouting together with an ominous repetitive thudding sound. There was no doubt in her mind that both Lucy and Violet were at immediate risk. Whoever was responsible for making the racket was way beyond angry.

'Jem? It's me, Lucy. I need you. I'm at Violet's house. There's some maniac outside trying to break the door down.'

Jemima felt a frisson of fear race down her spine. It was no longer just Violet who needed her protection. Her sister was currently in danger too. She wished that she had advised Lucy to stay away from Violet's house.

Even over the phone, Jemima could hear muffled shouts and the sound of something pounding against a surface. There was no point in advising Lucy and Violet to head out of the rear of the property, as it was surrounded on all sides by high fences. It would only mean that they'd be trapped in the garden with no means of escape. Their only viable option was to sit it out and wait for help to arrive.

'Arm yourselves with anything you can find,' Jemima told her. 'Push something up against the door. Make sure that every other means of access to the property is secure, then stay away from the door and windows. If possible, barricade yourself in an upstairs room. I'll request any officer in your area to attend immediately. Sit tight, I'm on my way.'

Jemima was already grabbing her things as she spoke. As she looked across at Broadbent, she saw that he was doing the same. There was no question that at least for now they were acting as a team.

CHAPTER 10

From the sound of the commotion, there was no time to lose, as whoever was trying to gain access to Violet's house was clearly losing it. Jemima and Broadbent raced along the corridor, down the stairs and out to the car. Jemima flung open the door and flicked on the siren and flashing lights as she turned the key to start the engine.

'Get on the radio and arrange for any units closer than us to attend,' ordered Jemima. 'Inform them that there's a possible threat to life.'

As they pulled into Violet's street, Jemima was surprised to discover that the area appeared deserted. There were no groups of nosey neighbours, keen to watch what was going down. And there was no police presence. As they approached the front door, a scraping noise could be heard coming from inside.

'Lucy, it's me, Jem. Open up,' Jemima called.

'Hang on, I'm just dragging some furniture out of the way,' came the reply.

When the door eventually opened, Jemima was shocked to witness the haunted expression on her sister's face. Lucy usually exuded confidence. It was self-assurance that had been nurtured and had subsequently flourished through a lifetime of being the favoured child.

'May we come in?' asked Jemima.

'Y-yes, sure.' Lucy stood aside to allow them to pass.

They headed down the narrow passageway towards the lounge, where they found Violet huddled on the sofa. Her feet were off the floor, knees touching her chin. With her arms wrapped tightly around her shins, the knuckles on her hands were white and prominent. She raised her head as they approached, and Jemima saw that she was crying.

'You can relax. There's no one out there,' said Jemima in an attempt to reassure Violet. 'This is Detective Constable Dan Broadbent. He's working this case with me.'

'Do you mind if I take a look around to make sure that everywhere is secure?' asked Broadbent.

'Sure,' agreed Violet.

'It's all quiet out there now, but what exactly happened?' asked Jemima. She perched on the arm of a chair and took notes as Violet spoke.

'I was about to open a bottle of wine when the doorbell sounded. I looked through the window, saw it was Byron, and didn't answer the door. He must have spotted me because he gave up ringing the doorbell and began hammering on the door. When that didn't work, I think he started kicking it too.'

'Did you actually see whoever was doing this?' asked Jemima, turning her attention to Lucy.

'No,' Lucy replied. 'Violet had already filled me in on what that creep was like, so as soon as it all kicked off, I got on the phone to you. After you told me to try to barricade the door, I grabbed one of the bar stools and dragged it out there to jam it under the door handle. It wasn't much, but it was all I could think of using. I lost it, Jem. I love to think of myself as being so clever and confident. But at the first sign of a crisis, I bloody lost it. I was useless.' Lucy began to cry too.

Jemima gave her sister a supportive hug. Lucy's admission of not having seen whoever had done this meant that so far there was no independent witness. Unless one of the neighbours could corroborate the allegation, when they spoke to Byron, it would undoubtedly be Violet's word against his.

'You're so brave, Jem. I've never really thought about it until now, but you're the one who puts herself out there day in, day out, facing down danger and protecting people. It's unbelievable that I haven't appreciated just what a hero you are.'

'It's just a job, Luce. Nothing more,' Jemima replied modestly. She was accustomed to her sister looking down her nose at her and, though the unanticipated compliment was welcome, it was a somewhat disconcerting turn of events, and would undoubtedly be short-lived.

'Are you going to arrest him?' asked Violet.

'We'll interview Mr Toombes about the incident and advise him to stay away from you,' said Jemima. 'We'll speak to the neighbours and see if they can verify your version of events. Unfortunately, there's very little we can do unless we have hard evidence against him. In cases like this, it often comes down to his word against yours, but I'll also advise him that we suspect him of harassment. Especially as this incident follows on from him approaching you yesterday when you told him to leave you alone. The problem comes if he's stalking you. If that's the case, having a word with him is unlikely to make him stop. So don't get your hopes up just yet.'

'Vi's not making it up. This guy's a creepy stalker. You've got to do something about it,' pleaded Lucy.

'I don't doubt anything that's been alleged. But the law operates on provable facts, otherwise anyone could become a victim of a hate campaign, simply because someone has it in for them. There has to be a burden of proof. So as I said yesterday, I suggest you keep a written record of any unwanted contact with Mr Toombes.'

'What else should I do?' asked Violet.

'We'll advise you on improved home security. You should carry a personal safety alarm so that you can set it off if he comes near you.'

'Does that mean you think he's going to attack me?' squealed Violet.

'I've no idea what he's capable of. Look, I'm not trying to scare you, Violet. I'm just making you aware of the worst-case scenario and suggesting things you can do to increase your chances of staying safe. If you were to find yourself in a vulnerable situation, then setting off a personal safety alarm could shock him sufficiently to buy you a few seconds to escape. As soon as you set the alarm off, you should run towards people and attract their attention by shouting and screaming as loudly as you possibly can. Don't be shy about it. You need people to take notice of you. That way, Toombes, or any other attacker is more likely to back off.

'Until we've had a chance to speak with him, I can't second-guess what we're dealing with. But you have to understand that if Byron Toombes is obsessed with you, he's not going to give up. Any contact you have with him won't be like interacting with a normal person. He'll want your attention and will do anything to get it. He'll want you to be thinking about him as much as he's obsessing about you.

'Social niceties, such as respecting the other person's wishes, don't exist with stalkers. You'll be the sole focus of his life. The reason he gets up in the morning, and the person he spends every waking moment thinking about. He'll believe he has a relationship with you, and he'll do anything to get closer to you. Whether you want him to or not.'

'We don't have a relationship,' countered Violet. 'He's just some creep I have the misfortune to live next door to.'

'I agree,' said Jemima. She reached out to squeeze Violet's hand, in what she hoped was a reassuring gesture. 'But as I've said, this man might not see it that way. It's conceivable that he believes he's in a relationship with you. If that's the case, nothing you do or say will shake that belief. You can't treat him like you would anyone else, because standard rules of behaviour don't apply. You can tell him to stay away until you're blue in the face. You can yell at him, threaten him with a court order, parade a string of lovers in front of him, but if he's obsessed with you, he won't accept that he means nothing to you. He's delusional. You can't change the way he

53

thinks of you. He'll crave your attention. He wants to be the focus of your life, just as you've become the focus of his. So the best thing you can do is to refuse to have any interaction with him whatsoever. Ideally it would be best if you could put some distance between yourself and him. Perhaps you could move to another rental property?'

'I can't just walk away. I've only recently signed a lease on this place,' said Violet.

'How long for?' asked Jemima.

'A year — I'm barely four months into it,' said Violet.

'Luce, could Violet stay at yours for a few days?' asked Jemima, turning her attention to her sister.

'Of course she can.'

'You need to put some distance between you and Byron Toombes. Even for a short while. Give us time to talk with him and take some statements from the neighbours. We'll be better placed to judge the situation in a couple of days' time. Now go and pack a bag,' ordered Jemima.

CHAPTER 11

'South Wales Police. Open up, Mr Toombes!' yelled Jemima, as she hammered on his door. She'd already tried the doorbell, keeping the button depressed to ensure that there would be no let-up of the sound inside the property. She could hear its tinny tones from where she stood on the pavement. It should have been enough to drive Byron Toombes to distraction, but it was clear that if he was inside, he had no intention of answering the door.

'I can't see anything through the window,' said Broadbent, as he stepped away from the glass. 'The blinds are shut, and there's no sign of light or life inside. Could be he's not there.'

'Oh, he's there all right,' snapped Jemima. 'He'll be keen to keep an eye on Violet. He's just too much of a coward to come out and face us.'

Jemima appreciated that at this moment there was little point in continuing to try to get Toombes to answer the door. As much as she would have liked to have a face-to-face confrontation with him, she was confident he wouldn't oblige, and as there was insufficient evidence, they needed to find someone who could independently identify Byron as having been the person who intimidated Violet. As things stood, their time would be better spent speaking to some of the neighbours, who would hopefully be able to corroborate Violet's version of events.

As they walked away from the property, Lucy and Violet came out to their respective vehicles. Violet was dragging a small case.

'What did he have to say for himself?' she asked.

'We haven't spoken to him yet,' said Jemima. 'He didn't answer the door.'

'Can't you get a warrant or something?' asked Violet.

'It doesn't work like that. From what you've told us, he's scared you. But he hasn't physically harmed you. We need to build a case against him.'

'So you're not even going to question him?' asked Violet. It was impossible not to pick up on her sense of incredulity.

'I assure you that we will, but not immediately. Go to Lucy's for a few days. I'll be in touch. We are taking this seriously, but it doesn't mean that we'll be able to stop him.'

'He's in there. I know he is. That's his car,' said Violet, pointing at the vehicle parked directly in front of his house.

Jemima glanced across at Lucy and spotted a mixture of anger and disappointment on her face. Lucy scowled and shook her head disapprovingly. So much for the few words of praise she had heaped upon Jemima only a few minutes earlier.

Jemima hated herself for dashing Violet's hopes, but she felt it was better to reinforce the reality check. It would help her manage her expectations about the likely outcome of this scary situation.

As the two women drove away, Jemima turned to find Broadbent already speaking with Violet's other next-door neighbour, Freida Holden.

As Freida leaned wearily against the door frame, a safety gate was visible, blocking an internal doorway. It prevented three small boys from escaping what appeared to be their playroom. Broadbent was forced to speak loudly to be heard over the constant shrieks, howls and laughter.

'Are they always this lively?' he inquired.

'Only when they're awake. The little darlings have far too much energy and keep egging each other on. Still, I wouldn't want to be without them. Though I'm counting down the days until they get their free nursery places. Hopefully, I'll start to feel human again. My husband, Joey, does his best to help out, but he works full-time and takes all the overtime they can give him. We're on a shoestring budget until I can return to work part-time.'

'Did you witness a commotion next door?' asked Jemima as she joined Broadbent.

'No. What happened? I wouldn't notice if a nuclear bomb went off. You can hear what my kids are like at the moment. And that's them being well behaved. It's like a warzone in there. We haven't ventured outside today.'

'Are you able to tell us anything about Byron Toombes?' pressed Jemima.

'Who?' asked Freida with a blank stare.

'Your neighbour, two doors down from here.'

'Oh, him. Bit of an oddball. A loner. He already lived there when we moved in, so that's at least four years ago. Don't get a good vibe from him, though,' said Freida.

'What do you mean?' asked Jemima.

'I don't know. Can't put my finger on it. There's just something about the man. Joey's not keen on him either, and he doesn't usually have a bad word to say about anyone.'

At that moment, there was a crash immediately followed by a piercing scream.

'Sorry, I've gotta go,' said Freida, as she lurched towards the safety gate and slammed the front door behind her.

'I suppose we can try some of the other neighbours,' said Broadbent.

They spent the following hour knocking on doors to establish whether anyone had seen or heard the disturbance at Violet's house. It had been a reasonable assumption that the occupants of the properties on the opposite side of the road would have had the best view of the incident, but they were unable to help. A district nurse arrived as they knocked on one of the doors and explained that the householder was bedridden and spent his time in a room at the back of the house.

The family in the adjoining house said they had never spoken to Toombes or Violet and they informed Jemima that the couple who owned the other house were away on holiday.

Jemima and Broadbent headed back to Toombes's house to find that it was still in darkness. Jemima pressed the bell and repeatedly knocked on the door, but there was no sign of life inside. It was frustrating yet unsurprising. Toombes was clearly a person who liked to be in control of things, but he would have to speak with them sooner or later.

Jemima returned to the car and wrote a note telling Toombes to report to the station to attend an interview. She pushed it through the letterbox, knowing that if he failed to contact her by the morning, things would become a whole lot more serious for him.

CHAPTER 12

Early the following morning, Jemima arrived at her sister's apartment to speak to Violet before she went to work. Lucy opened the door and stood aside to allow Jemima to enter. There was no welcoming smile or the offer of a cup of coffee. It didn't take a genius to realize that Lucy was still annoyed.

At first sight, Violet appeared more relaxed, though Jemima quickly realized that it was all an act. As there was an undeniable tremor in Violet's hands as she lifted a mug of steaming coffee to her lips.

'Did you manage to get any sleep?' asked Jemima.

'Some,' replied Violet. 'What did he have to say for himself?' The usually polite Violet was fading away as the strain. She had no time for pleasantries — she was under the narrowed focus of a man who wanted to become the centre of her universe. She wanted nothing to do with Byron. Yet he had succeeded in becoming the most important person in her world. He was waging a war. He had invaded her thoughts while she was awake, and certainly occupied her mind while she slept. Instead of living her life he had got her marching to the beat of his drum.

'We haven't interviewed Byron Toombes yet,' said Jemima.

'I thought you were going to take this seriously?' snapped Lucy. She made no attempt to disguise her anger.

Jemima was in no doubt that the question was a dig at her professionalism. 'I am taking this seriously,' she replied. 'Perhaps you'd like to take yourself off to work so that I can speak with Violet alone?'

'I don't need to leave yet. You seem to have forgotten that you're in my home. Don't try to tell me what to do.'

It was almost as if they'd stepped back in time and reverted to being teenagers again. In a matter of seconds, all the old sibling rivalry and resentments resurfaced. Jemima half expected Lucy to grab hold of her hair and wrestle her to the ground, the way they'd often settled their differences when they shared a bedroom. But Jemima didn't have the time or the inclination to rise to the bait. She had a long day ahead of her, and this was just the start of her shift. She ignored her sister and spoke directly to Violet.

'We made numerous attempts to get hold of Mr Toombes last night. Unfortunately, we couldn't get an answer when we called at the property. There was nothing to suggest that he was at home, as the place was in darkness. And as I explained yesterday, we didn't have the right to force an entry. I left a note for him to make arrangements to attend the station. I checked before I set off from home and he hadn't been in touch, so I've asked a uniformed officer to call round there. Hopefully, they'll catch him before he goes to work. If he's there, he'll be taken to the station, where I'll question him about the allegations you've made.'

'What if he's not?' asked Violet.

'Then we'll go to his place of work. But we will speak to him.'

'Good,' said Violet.

'Are you going to work today?'

'Yes,' said Violet.

'And does Toombes know where you work?'

'Yes.'

'Is there anyone who could give you a lift?'

'S'pose so.'

'Good. Until we know what we're dealing with, it's safer for you to be with other people. And stay inside at lunchtime. It's just a precaution, but better safe than sorry. I'll be in touch when I have more information.'

* * *

Jemima arrived at the station to discover that there had been no sign of Byron Toombes at his home. As his car had been outside the house on the previous evening, it was apparent that he'd ignored Jemima's note advising him to contact the station. It was a reckless approach, given that he worked alongside the police. The man was pushing his luck, and she could feel her anger about to spill over.

'Toombes thinks he's so smart avoiding us like this,' said Jemima, as she put on her jacket and grabbed the car keys. 'But he's messing with the wrong woman. He's overstepped the mark by ignoring the note I shoved through the letter-box. He seems to think he's above the law, probably because his job requires him to have regular contact with the police. Well, let's see how he likes it when he's hauled out of work in front of his colleagues.'

'Too right.' Broadbent followed her out of the door.

* * *

Jemima breathed a sigh of relief as they pulled up outside the SOCO office. She was thankful traffic had been light and the journey not too long. It was becoming easier spending time alone with Broadbent now he was no longer overtly hostile. They still had a long way to go to feel completely comfortable with each other, but at the moment professional courtesy was a considerable improvement on the way things had been between them.

'We're looking for Byron Toombes,' said Jemima, as they showed the receptionist their warrant cards.

'Is he expecting you?' asked the young man behind the desk.

'He should be,' said Jemima.

'Could I tell him what it's about?' pressed the receptionist. It was evident from the eagerness in his voice that he was keen to learn some gossip.

'No. Just direct us to his workstation. We'll take it from here, and do not under any circumstances ring ahead to say that we're on our way,' ordered Jemima. She gave the man a steely stare to emphasize that she was not to be messed with.

The receptionist compliantly stammered his way through a set of directions, which ultimately led them to a small open-plan office on the third floor of the building.

As soon as they entered the room, a middle-aged woman approached to challenge them.

'Excuse me, do you have an appointment?' she asked, stepping directly in front of them to halt their progress.

'We're police officers,' said Jemima, holding out her warrant card. 'We're looking for Byron Toombes.'

'Is it about one of the crime scenes he's attended?' the woman inquired.

Jemima had no intention of answering the question and fixed the woman with a withering gaze.

'His desk is on the far side of the room,' the woman said eventually. 'I'll take you there.'

As they headed through the office, people raised their heads, and an audible whisper followed in their wake. As they reached Toombes's desk, he looked up, sensing someone was there.

'Mr Toombes, we'd like you to accompany us to the police station to answer some questions about an incident which occurred yesterday evening,' said Jemima. As she cautioned him, her words rang out loudly. It was her intention to let everyone know that they were taking Byron Toombes in for questioning.

* * *

Throughout the journey to the police station, Toombes made no attempt to speak. Whenever Jemima glanced at him in the rear-view mirror, his eyes were closed, as though he was asleep or meditating. But he wasn't fooling her. Jemima knew from experience that he was using the time to rehearse his version of events.

Once inside the station, they took him to an interview room, where Toombes refused his right to a solicitor. He stuck to the line of having no need for legal representation as he hadn't done anything wrong.

'What is your relationship with Violet Watkins?' asked Jemima.

'She's a friend and neighbour,' replied Toombes.

'What exactly do you mean by the term "friend"?' pressed Jemima.

'Isn't it obvious? Or are you that sad that you don't have any friends?'

'Stop wasting my time, Mr Toombes. I'm not playing games here. Tell me about your so-called friendship with Violet Watkins,' continued Jemima. She already disliked this man and was determined not to let him get the upper hand by deflecting and scoring cheap points. People like Toombes needed to feel in control of things. While he thought he was calling the shots, the mask he presented to the world would remain firmly in place. Jemima needed to wrong-foot him in the hope that the real Byron Toombes would reveal himself. Toombes had declined the services of a solicitor, meaning the odds had shifted against him.

'What's this about?' Toombes asked. 'You'd better have a good reason for dragging me out of work and embarrassing me in front of my colleagues. You rely on us to work alongside you. So a bit of professional courtesy wouldn't go amiss.' As he settled back in the chair, the weight of his body caused the flimsy seat to slide backwards, and the legs grated noisily across the floor. He appeared far too comfortable. But, despite the cool temperature in the room, Jemima spotted sweat stains on his shirt. It was a telltale sign that beneath the bravado, Toombes was still feeling the pressure.

'You're looking rather hot and bothered, Mr Toombes. We're just getting started. If you lie to us, the pressure will only get worse, because you'll be forced to elaborate upon that lie. And the further you travel down that particular road, the more opportunities you'll present us with to catch you out.'

'On the contrary, I feel fine,' he replied. 'I've no need to lie. In fact, it's quite exciting. Things like this don't usually happen to people like me. I'll be able to dine out on this experience for quite a while. So come on, tell me, what's this all about? What on earth do you think I've done?'

'Miss Watkins claims that you've been harassing her. I witnessed you approach her the other day and advised you to stay away from her. But it seems as though you didn't heed my advice. She said that, amongst other things, you called around to her house yesterday. When she refused to open the door, you hammered on it for a sustained period with such force that she thought the door was going to give way. She also said that you shouted threats and abuse, which made her fear for her safety.'

'That's not what happened. Violet's twisting the truth,' Toombes replied, in a calm and even tone.

'So what exactly did happen, Mr Toombes?'

'It's true that I called around. But you must understand the background leading up to it. You see, Violet and I have a chequered history. On the day she moved in next door, I called around to welcome her to her new home. I'd not met her before, and at the time, I had no idea of what she was like or the emotional baggage that came with her. She opened up about a recently failed long-term relationship, but what I didn't expect was for her to just hit on me. I thought it could be a rebound thing. But whatever the reason, she had no intention of letting the grass grow under her feet. If I'm honest about it, I was shocked, because women don't usually throw themselves at me.

'It didn't help that I was particularly vulnerable at the time. You see, I'd reached a low point in my life. Both of my parents had recently died, and I was struggling. From the moment Violet moved in, she needed help. She was on her own, there were lots of things to be done, and I was grateful for the distraction. It got me through a very dark time. It suited us both.'

'So you were just being neighbourly?' asked Broadbent, shaking his head in disbelief.

'That's right, but I soon came to realize that Violet wanted more than just help with practical things. She wanted a relationship with all the bells and whistles. But I wasn't ready for that sort of commitment, and I told her so. I was reeling from my parents' deaths. It was a brutal way to lose them. One moment they were alive. The next they were gone. It hit me for six, and I still haven't fully recovered from it. I'm not in the right headspace to commit to any sort of relationship at the moment. I'm still trying to get my own life back on track.

'I was upfront and honest with Violet. I told her that I wasn't interested in anything other than a platonic relationship. She's not my type. I know plenty of people would think she's an attractive woman. I'm just not one of them.

'Anyway, we muddled along for a while, spending the occasional evening together, sometimes sharing a meal. But it all fell apart when Violet had a housewarming party, and I ended up getting off with her colleague, Tania. Now, that woman was definitely my type. She was a right little minx. We'd been drinking when she sat on my lap and began to gyrate to the music. You can imagine the effect she had on me. Any man would have done the same.' Toombes directed his last comment towards Broadbent.

Jemima spoke loudly to interrupt Toombes's flow. 'This anecdote has no bearing whatsoever on the incident we're investigating,' she said.

'Yes, it does,' countered Toombes.

'How so?' asked Broadbent.

'Long story short, we headed upstairs. One thing led to another, and Violet caught us in flagrante. It was embarrassing.

Violet went ape, and there's been no reasoning with her since. I feel bad about it, and I've tried to get our friendship back on track. But Violet's treating it as though I cheated on her. Yet we've never been in a relationship with each other.'

'So, why not just avoid her from then on?' asked Jemima.

'Honestly? I suppose it's because I've been through so much in the last few months. Losing my parents has made me realize that life's too short to hold grudges. Violet and I live next door to each other. The way I see it, we're better off rubbing along with each other.

'Last night was my latest ham-fisted attempt to get back into her good books. I admit that I took things too far. But I've tried everything I can think of to make things right with her. I was just so frustrated that she's not prepared to put the incident behind her and move on. I probably did shout some horrible things, and I definitely hammered on the door. Take a look at my hand. It's bruised,' said Toombes, holding it out for them to inspect. 'But there wasn't any sinister motive behind my actions. I just feel awful about what happened at that party. I want Violet's forgiveness so that we can move on from the whole sorry episode.'

'So you deny harassing Violet Watkins?' pressed Jemima.

'Of course I do. I'm just trying to make amends for my bad behaviour at the party. That's all there is to it.'

'Did you realize that there was someone with Violet last night, when you called around to the house?' pressed Jemima.

'Yes, I thought I saw someone. Whoever it was should be able to verify what I've just said. If I'd wanted to break that door down, I'm sure I could have. But I didn't. I was just frustrated that Violet won't forgive me. The fact that she's made an official complaint changes everything. Violet obviously has no intention of putting the incident behind us, so I'll avoid her at all costs from now on.'

'Make sure you do. Get it into your head that Violet Watkins wants nothing to do with you, and the law is on her side in this matter. From now on, you don't look at her, you don't even breathe in her direction, because if you continue harassing her, I'll advise Miss Watkins to take out an injunction against you, and that could mean that you'll have to stay away from your own house. Have I made myself clear?'

'Yes. Tell Violet from me that there's no reason for her to be afraid. I'll leave her alone. I won't even acknowledge her if our paths cross. She needs to accept that we might occasionally bump into each other. It's inevitable. We live next-door to each other. But, hand on heart, I'll do everything in my power to avoid her,' said Toombes, theatrically placing his hand on his chest to emphasize his sincerity.

Jemima's instinct told her that Byron Toombes was lying to them, but having heard his explanation for the recent events, she realized that there was no evidence to prove that he had twisted the truth. Lucy had witnessed Toombes's outburst, but it could easily be explained away just as the man himself had done. No harm had come to Violet, despite her obvious fear of Toombes. As things stood, there was no case to answer.

'Very well, Mr Toombes, you're free to leave. But stay away from Violet Watkins, or things will get very messy for you. Do I make myself clear?' Jemima gave him a steely stare. She was determined he would know that she was not a woman he could mess with.

'Perfectly,' he replied. As he stood up to leave, the faintest hint of a smile played across his lips.

CHAPTER 13

Byron Toombes sauntered out of the interview room, looking far more confident than when they had brought him in for questioning. The man had clearly been shaken when they confronted him at work. Jemima had studied him carefully. His upper body tensed the moment he became aware of their presence. Being caught off-guard was an uncomfortable experience for anyone. For a control freak, it would be an excruciatingly humiliating experience.

The way they hauled him in for questioning should have been enough to keep him on the back foot. Given a similar set of circumstances, many people would have crumbled, but somehow, Toombes had managed to dig deep and explain away the accusations thrown at him.

Jemima's opinion of Toombes was coloured by having witnessed the recent encounter in the coffee shop, and her subsequent conversations with Catrin and Stella. If she had gone into this interview cold, she might have thought differently of him. It was a worrying thought that he could explain away his behaviour and make his actions sound so reasonable. It was already abundantly clear from this first official encounter that they were dealing with a man who was intelligent enough to stay at least one step ahead.

Jemima grimaced as a knot of frustration tightened in her gut. She knew precisely what Toombes was up to, yet she lacked the proof that would enable her to stop him. This man wasn't going to back off. He clearly enjoyed playing games and had no intention of losing. Which made him dangerous.

'This isn't going to be easy,' said Broadbent. 'Toombes has an answer for everything and knows our procedures inside out.'

'Which is why we need to up our game,' said Jemima. 'A man like him always has to win, no matter the cost. It's part of his psyche. I don't believe that he's willingly going to walk away and leave Violet alone, so we're going to have to do something about it. We need to box him in. Find out everything we can about him, so we know exactly what we're up against, then shut him down once and for all.'

'Easier said than done,' said Broadbent.

'I don't want to hear it. There's no room on this team for a defeatist attitude. Toombes is a dangerous predator, and we're going to do everything in our power to take him down. What have the background checks you were working on thrown up?'

'Not a lot so far. The only things I've discovered are that he doesn't have a criminal record, which isn't surprising given his job. There's one coincidence, though. He's living in a property owned by the same company who own Violet's house.'

'That's interesting but perhaps not surprising. Let's face it, a lot of landlords own multiple properties and set up small companies for tax purposes. Make a note of the company name along with the details of the directors. Have you established where he was born and brought up?'

'Not yet,' said Broadbent.

'You're going to have to speed up and become more proactive, Dan. Especially on a case like this, when a young woman's relying on us to keep her safe.'

'I'm doing the best I can,' snapped Broadbent, unable to keep the irritation from spilling over into his voice.

'Are you? Are you really?' Jemima arched her eyebrows in disbelief. 'I tell you what, why not do some basic admin-type tasks? Ease yourself in. After all, I don't want you over-doing things.'

'There's no need to be like that.'

'We don't have time for this. Why don't you make a series of appointments for tomorrow afternoon, so that we can speak to Toombes's work colleagues on an individual basis? Perhaps that may open up a few more avenues for us. Don't tell them what it's about, though. I'll also give you the names of people working with Violet. We'll need to speak with them too, ideally in the morning. In the meantime, I'll take on the task of finding out more about Byron. I'll start with social media to see if anything comes up.'

* * *

After work, Jemima made a detour to her sister's apartment. She'd spent much of the day battling a growing sense of anger. It had begun as she watched Byron Toombes saunter out of the interview room without any charge being brought against him. It frequently felt that as a police officer, you had to operate with both hands tied behind your back. Your job was to uphold the law and protect the public. Yet even when you had a strong sense of how a particular situation would play out, you still couldn't do anything about it. Everything was weighted in favour of the criminals.

Jemima was convinced that Toombes had played them. But as there was no evidence to prove any wrongdoing, they were unable to charge him. It rankled. She had the option of breaking the news to Violet over the phone, but that would have been the coward's way out, and Jemima believed that the least she could do was to have a face-to-face conversation with her.

When Lucy answered the door, it was clear that she was still in a frosty mood. Jemima muttered a half-hearted greet-ing as she headed inside but couldn't bring herself to make eye contact. There seemed little point in observing pleasantries, as she was sure that her sister would kick off as soon as she broke the news.

Jemima couldn't have felt more wretched when she saw that Violet's eyes were bright with optimism. The young woman eagerly searched Jemima's face, expecting to be told that her troubles were behind her. It was a naivety police officers frequently witnessed, as it was human nature to hope that things would get better.

Childhood fairy tales had a lot to answer for. So many people seemed to believe that there was a magic wand to make things better and that in the end, good would triumph over evil. If only . . .

'Have you arrested him?' asked Violet. The words tumbled out of her mouth in her eagerness to be told the good news.

'I'm afraid not. We brought Byron in for questioning, but he gave a plausible account of what happened yesterday,' began Jemima.

'You believe him over me?' asked Violet. Her eyes widened with disbelief and shock. The incredulity in her voice cut Jemima to the quick.

'No, I don't. It's got—' began Jemima.

'You really are unbelievable!' snapped Lucy. 'I called you because you're my sister. I thought you'd go the extra mile. Believe our version of events. But instead, you chose to take his side.'

'It's not about sides, Luce. It's about what we can or cannot prove. We can only operate within the confines of the law. Byron Toombes gave a plausible explanation for his actions. He's not contradicting what happened. But he explained the motive for his actions last night.'

'Save it, Jem! You're bloody useless,' said Lucy.

'For what it's worth, I don't believe that he was telling us the truth. But at the moment I'm unable to prove otherwise. If we could arrest people on gut feelings, we'd have more people in prison than walking around free.'

'What am I supposed to do now?' squealed Violet. She suddenly looked small and extremely vulnerable, having scooted back on the sofa, allowing the cushions virtually to swallow her up.

'I've warned Byron Toombes to stay away from you. If he gives you any cause for concern, then get in touch with me immediately. We'll treat it as harassment, possibly even stalking. If you decide to return home, there are things you can do to make the property more secure. But either you or your landlord will have to foot the bill. I've got contact details for a trustworthy professional who's able to fit additional locks to your windows and doors, along with door chains and a spy hole. She also provides panic buttons, and if your budget allows, you can have them linked to the police station.

'My earlier advice still stands. Record any interactions, suspicious events, or threatening behaviour in as much detail as possible, along with dates and times. Also make a note of any witnesses, as it will help further down the line.

'As far as possible, don't be predictable in the way you live your life. I know it's difficult if you have regular working hours, but try to mix things up a bit so that he doesn't expect you to do things at a particular time. And as I mentioned yesterday, get a personal safety alarm. Learn how to operate it and make sure you carry it with you at all times.'

'What about getting a lodger?' asked Lucy.

'That's a good idea, as long as it's someone Violet knows and trusts. Though I'd suggest that if you're thinking of going down that route, you check the terms of your rental agreement first,' said Jemima.

'I will. And I suppose I could ask around at work,' said Violet. 'See if anyone's interested. There's plenty of space, and the extra money would come in useful. Having someone share the house with me should help me feel safe. But if they get wind of what's been happening, I doubt anyone would want to move in. After all, who would want to live next door to a creep like him?'

'On that note, you should know that I've made appointments to speak with everyone who attended the gathering at your house. It's a fact-finding exercise as much as anything. We may get lucky and discover that Byron let some useful information slip. After all, you said that everyone was drinking, so his guard would have been down. So don't be surprised when you see me at your workplace tomorrow.'

'Well, thanks a lot. Once you've spoken to them, I won't stand any chance of getting one of them to move in with me.'

'You don't know that, and it's not as if I'm doing it out of spite. If we're going to stand any chance of building a case against Toombes, I need to gather as much information as I can about him. And you're not stuck at that property, Violet. You can always move in with your grandparents.'

'But I don't want to. Why should I have my whole life turned upside down?'

'Because life's not fair. Sometimes it's sensible to cut your losses and walk away while you still can. In the meantime, if Lucy's happy for you to stay, then give it a few days before you think of moving back. Ideally, sort out the security upgrades first. Your absence should give Toombes a chance to get a better perspective on things too. But remember, I'm just a phone call away if you need help.'

CHAPTER 14

The previous twelve months had seen significant changes occur in Jemima's life. Almost two years earlier, Jemima had met her now-husband Nick Huxley by chance at a Cardiff Blues home game. Jemima had reluctantly been dragged along to the rugby match by a couple of friends, and Nick had been attending the game in his capacity as a sports correspondent with the *Daily Wales* newspaper. During the interval, as Jemima made her way from the restroom, the strap on her shoulder bag snapped, sending it tumbling to the ground. She had vaguely been aware of someone walking towards her but thought no more of it as she bent down to retrieve her bag. Unbeknown to her, the man now only a few feet away saw what had happened and gallantly bent down to retrieve the bag at the exact same moment as Jemima. Their skulls inevitably collided. As they both rubbed their heads and stared at each other, there was an undeniable instant attraction.

Jemima was drawn towards Nick's unmistakable joie de vivre. He was funny, kind, relaxed and open — in stark contrast to some members of her own family. For once in her life, she felt loved, appreciated and accepted for who she was. It was such a refreshing change.

Nick had just come out of an unhappy marriage and had a young son, James. After three months, Nick introduced Jemima to his son and was delighted to discover that they were happy to spend time together. Jemima bonded effortlessly with the boy, even though James wasn't her child, and it was soon apparent that James favoured Jemima, often choosing to hold her hand or sit on her lap, instead of his father's.

Apart from James, Nick had no family. In contrast, Jemima had her parents — Donald and Celia Goodman, as well as a sister, Lucy. Though, despite having family members who lived nearby, Jemima had learned to keep her distance. To the outside world, the Goodmans appeared to be the perfect family unit. It was an illusion created and encouraged by Celia Goodman. It was important to Celia that her children were exemplary in every way, as her daughters were a reflection of her capability as a mother.

A family member's success was ultimately her success. And it quickly became apparent that of the two children, Lucy was going to be the high-achiever. Jemima was intelligent but displayed a tendency early on to be a free spirit, and that was not an attribute her mother had wished to encourage.

From the time Jemima was a toddler, Celia set out to break her daughter's spirit. In public, Celia expertly played the part of the long-suffering mother having to keep a firm hand on her wayward child, but on those occasions when there was just the two of them, things often took a sinister turn. Jemima was kept in line with frequent emotional and occasional physical abuse. Celia's favoured form of punishment was to grab a handful of Jemima's hair and pull her close, while grinding the knuckles of her free hand into Jemima's scalp. It was incredibly painful but ensured that the bruises didn't show.

Despite being desperate to please, nothing Jemima did was ever good enough to win genuine praise from her mother, and, unsurprisingly, Celia Goodman's parenting had an adverse effect on Jemima. Jemima learned early on in life that she could not take her mother's love for granted. Occasionally, she dared to ask why Lucy was being treated more favourably, and she was invariably punished for questioning her mother's motives. Celia unashamedly brainwashed both her children into believing that one of them deserved better treatment than the other.

Despite having lived independently for many years, Jemima still felt nauseous whenever she thought of her childhood. Her mother's favourite mantra was that everyone gets what they deserve in life, as good things happen to good people. Jemima had lost count of the number of times her mother had used that saying to explain away Lucy's privileged treatment.

It was only when Jemima moved out of the family home that she came to appreciate that her mother's behaviour was far from ordinary. It was a shocking and liberating realization, though one she felt unable to share with either her father or her sister. They both remained seemingly oblivious to Celia's true nature. Jemima instinctively knew that there was no point in talking things over with her father or Lucy, as neither of them would believe what she had to say. So instead, Jemima forged her own path in life. It was a lonely but necessary choice, though she did have occasional contact with her sister and sometimes telephoned her father while he was at work.

And so, Jemima married Nick Huxley in secret. It was not how she had imagined her wedding day would be, but it was perfect nevertheless.

They were five weeks into their marriage when Jemima heard the news that she had been offered a sergeant's post. Two weeks before she took up the position, she and Nick had moved into their first house together. Their new home was a three-bed semi in a quiet cul-de-sac in Thornhill, a popular housing development to the north of the city.

* * *

When Jemima arrived home that evening, she was delighted to discover that James was there. Nick's ex-wife Wendy had dropped their son off at short notice. It was something she was increasingly in the habit of doing.

As Jemima headed towards the kitchen, she heard the soundtrack of *Peppa Pig* playing in the lounge. It was currently one of James's favourite DVDs, guaranteed to keep him occupied if they needed to get on with other things.

'What was Wendy's excuse this time?' Jemima asked.

Nick stopped chopping onions and turned to kiss her. 'Apparently she just fancied a night out. She told me she'd pick him up before I go to work tomorrow.'

'Well at least we get to spend some extra time with him,' said Jemima. The truth was she loved having James come to stay with them. It allowed her to be a doting parent without having the day-to-day responsibility of having a child of her own.

James was a welcome distraction from the ugliness Jemima encountered in her job. Whenever he was around, there was no danger of her thoughts dwelling on what had happened at work. Time spent with James was a whirlwind of fun and laughter. Unless he was overtired, at which point grumpiness kicked in big time.

'How long until dinner's ready?' Jemima asked.

'About an hour. I've already fed James. Are you up for giving him a bath? I think he's beginning to get tired.'

'No probs. I'll read him a bedtime story too.'

'Thanks, Jem. You're the best.'

As Jemima poked her head around the door to the lounge, she could see James sitting on the sofa, clutching Jolly Tall. The giraffe was his favourite character from Jane Hissey's *Old Bear* books. It had become a ritual that whenever James stayed over, JT had to go to bed with him. Either Nick or Jemima had to read one of the stories, as James clutched the soft toy to his chest and invariably fell asleep before the end of the book.

Sensing someone entering the room, James turned his head and squealed in delight the moment he realized who was there. 'Mima! Mima! Mima!' he shouted, shuffling off the sofa and racing into her arms.

Jemima felt her heart skip a beat as she scooped him up and swung him around. She closed her eyes and hugged him tightly, determined to make the most of every second spent together. His breath was warm against her cheek as he gave her a sloppy kiss. She giggled uncontrollably as she snuggled against him.

'How's my little man?' she asked when she eventually came up for air.

'We watch *Peppa Pig*?' he asked.

'For a few minutes, but then it'll be bath time. I've bought more bubbles, and we'll play with your boats.'

'Yay!' he shouted enthusiastically, and as they both sat on the sofa he moulded his body against hers.

* * *

Later, a freshly bathed James lay in bed, grasping the giraffe as though his life depended upon it. Jemima sat next to him and read a story about Henry Isaiah, a bear so named because he had one eye higher than the other. The book was beautifully illustrated. As usual, James was mesmerized as he stared at the pictures while she read the words, ensuring that she altered her voice for each of the characters.

Jemima was only halfway through the story when James's breathing began to slow. His eyelids were clearly heavy, but he was determined to stay awake. With less than a page to go, his determination waned, and the lad finally lost the battle. As his eyes closed, he gave a little snuffle.

Jemima smiled and continued reading out loud until she finished the tale. She sighed contentedly as she closed the book and placed it gently on the shelf, before bending down to adjust the duvet. Gently sweeping a few strands of hair away from his eyes, she kissed him lightly on the forehead. Before she left the room, she turned off the bedside lamp and switched on the nightlight.

As Jemima was getting changed into joggers and a sweat-shirt, she heard Nick padding up the stairs.

'Dinner's ready in five,' he said in a hushed tone.

'Wonderful, I'm ravenous.'

At first, they ate in silence, both eagerly shovelling fork-fuls of food into their mouths. Nick was the first to speak.

'How'd it go with the lazy shit-stirrer?' He'd not had the opportunity to meet Daniel Broadbent, but he'd heard all about how he'd treated Jemima since she'd taken up the sergeant's post.

'He's mellowing. There's a definite thaw in hostilities since Kennedy had a word with him. At least there's a glimmer of hope that we'll be able to work together. I'm not kidding myself that it's going to be easy, but I think we're beginning to make some headway.'

'About time too. It makes my blood boil when I think about how that prick's treated you.'

'It's nice to know that you've got my back, but I'm a big girl. I can take everything he throws at me, and more.' Jemima couldn't help but smile as she reached out and squeezed his hand. It was comforting to know that her husband cared so much.

'I'll always have your back, Jem. We're a team, and always will be. I got the impression you seemed a bit down when you arrived?'

'I was, but it was nothing to do with Daniel Broadbent. It was Lucy. I had to call round to see someone who's staying with her at the moment. It's to do with a case I'm working on. I won't go into details, apart from saying that it's a par-ticularly tricky set of circumstances.'

'So tell me, what did Saint Lucy do to upset you?' he pressed.

'Oh, the usual. My sister has mastered the technique of making me feel inadequate.'

'Where do the women in your family get off? It seems as though you're the only decent one on the female side.'

'I think you're probably biased, Nick.'

'That's as maybe, but still . . .'

'Lucy's got her good points too. It's just unfortunate that she sometimes allows her opinion of me to be coloured by what she was brainwashed into believing when we were kids.'

'If you ask me, it's about time you set her straight.'

'There's no point. It really isn't worth the hassle. Lucy will believe what she wants to believe. If she's ever going to get to the stage of acknowledging the truth, then it'll have to be because she's opened her eyes and arrived at a conclusion by herself. She's not a stupid person. She'll realize it one day.'

'Yeah? Well, I'll take your word for that, Jem. She may very well be the only Oxford graduate in your family, but she's still an idiot who can't see the truth when it's staring her in the face.'

'I'll drink to that,' laughed Jemima, as she raised her glass and chinked it against her husband's.

CHAPTER 15

After speaking with DI Kennedy the following morning, it was agreed that Broadbent would continue with his task of trying to establish the owner of both Violet's and Byron's properties. Jemima was to head over to Violet's workplace to speak to colleagues who had attended the gathering at her home.

The organization that Violet worked for was based on the fifth floor of an office block, situated near the city's main shopping centre. It was a building that Jemima frequently passed but had not particularly noticed. Outside the main entrance was a list of all the businesses and organizations that were based in the building. As she scanned the names, Jemima noted that there were some well-known companies amongst its tenants.

The foyer seemed too modern and impressive for a non-profit charitable organization to choose as its headquarters. Everywhere Jemima looked, there was tinted glass and stainless steel.

A large reception desk was located directly opposite the entrance. It allowed the receptionist a view of the pavement, while ensuring that any visitors to the building would be spotted immediately. To the left of the reception area were two glass elevators, and as Jemima stepped towards them, a man in a grey suit suddenly blocked her way.

'Do you have a pass?' he asked. It seemed that even the security guard was better dressed than anyone Jemima usually came into contact with.

'No. I'm a police officer. I've arranged to speak to some people located on the fifth floor,' said Jemima, as she rummaged in her bag to find her warrant card.

'You'll need to sign in at reception. Someone will have to come down to escort you. There are some high-profile tenants in this building, so you can't just wander around. Their security is a top priority.'

'Glad to hear it,' said Jemima. Despite thinking that the man was a jumped-up oaf, it was reassuring to know that Toombes would be challenged should he ever try to access the building. It meant that at least this was a safe space for Violet — somewhere she could put the threat he posed to her safety to the back of her mind for a while.

It was almost ten minutes later when an intern arrived to collect Jemima. As he escorted her to the fifth floor, he chatted away relentlessly. At one stage Jemima thought of telling him to be quiet but soon realized that would be counterproductive. After all, she was there to get people to talk to her, and it wouldn't be the wisest move to kick things off on the wrong foot.

A small room had been made available for Jemima. It was of a similar size to police interview rooms, but that was where any direct comparison ended. The area, though small, was tastefully decorated with modern prints, plush carpeting and comfortable furniture.

The first member of staff that Jemima spoke to was Tania Lennon — the woman who had had sex with Toombes at Violet's home. Jemima's initial impression was that she was nervous and embarrassed. She was tall, young and undeniably pretty, and it was easy to imagine that she would draw a lot of male attention.

'As you're probably aware, I'm here because I'm making inquiries about Violet's neighbour, Byron Toombes. I understand this may very well be an uncomfortable experience for you. Still, I'd like you to be completely honest when you answer my questions. I'm not here to judge you. I'm just trying to build up a picture of Byron.'

'So you've obviously been told about what happened at Violet's house?' asked Tania, unable to look Jemima in the eye. She sat on the edge of the seat, addressing a spot on the floor.

'If you mean that you had sex with Byron, then yes. But I'm not interested in that. I just want to know anything you're able to tell me about him.'

'Is he dangerous or something?'

'It's a possibility.'

'Shit! I wish I hadn't gone to that fucking house,' said Tania. She began to cry. 'It was a party. I had too much to drink and was feeling sorry for myself. I was on the rebound because my boyfriend had just dumped me. It seemed like a good idea at the time. But now everyone hates me.'

'I'm sure no one hates you, Tania. At one time or another, everyone has done something they later regret. I don't wish to appear unsympathetic, but I do need you to tell me about Byron.'

Tania shuddered. 'I didn't think much of it at the time, but he seemed overly preoccupied with Violet. I remember when she walked into the lounge and saw that he was there, the expression on her face changed. She looked angry. He smiled at her and tried to touch her arm. She batted his hand away without acknowledging him. I thought at first that she was playing hard to get. But then I realized she was blanking him. She wasn't pleased to see him.

'I was on the voddy and hadn't had much to eat. I'd just helped myself to another when Byron started flirting with me. He wasn't really my type, but it felt good having someone pay me some attention. One thing led to another, and we headed upstairs, and you know the rest . . .'

'Was there anything he did or said which seemed strange or made you feel uncomfortable?'

'Now you mention it, he was insistent that I lie on one particular part of the bed. Violet's bed is quite large. I'd got on one side of it, but he insisted that I move over.'

'Towards the middle?' asked Jemima.

'No, that's the thing. It would have made more sense if Byron had wanted me to be in the middle of the bed, as it would have made things easier. For some reason, he insisted on us being on the other side of the bed. I didn't think anything of it at the time.'

'Was there anything else that seemed a bit off with him?'

'I can't be certain, but I think he might have swiped something of Violet's. I remember seeing a few bits of jewellery on the bedside table. One of them was a necklace with a gold heart, but I don't think it was there later. I mean when Violet came in and went ballistic.'

Jemima made a mental note to check with Violet whether or not she had lost the necklace. But what interested her most was Tania's assertion that Toombes had insisted on being on a particular part of the bed. It seemed unusual.

The only other surprising piece of information came from a woman named Tricia Forsyth. She told Jemima that Toombes had reacted strangely when she was about to examine an oddly placed screw in the lounge. She hadn't noticed it at first, as it almost blended in with the wallpaper, and could easily be mistaken for the stigma of a flower.

As Tricia had moved closer to have a better view, Toombes had barged in front of her and tipped red wine down her top. He'd apologized for his actions, claiming to have had too much to drink. But in retrospect, Tricia sensed that it might not have been the case.

When Jemima had finished speaking with everyone who had attended the event, she asked to see Violet.

A few minutes later, Violet walked into the room, carrying an armful of documents. 'Have you found out anything useful?'

'I'm not sure. I'd like to check out a few things at your house. Would it be possible for you to meet me there at six o'clock? Perhaps you could ask Lucy to come with you so that you won't have to go there on your own?'

'Sure. I'll see you at my place at six,' said Violet. She was already backing out of the room as she spoke.

* * *

When Jemima returned to the police station, Broadbent was examining various sheets of printed paper that were spread across his desk. As she moved closer, she realized they were a list of addresses, each with a date next to it. 'What've you got there?' she asked.

'Take a guess.'

'No idea. Please tell me that it's somehow linked to the inquiry and you haven't been dragged off to do something else.'

'It is linked. I don't know if it helps, though my gut tells me it probably doesn't,' said Broadbent, as he reached out and quickly gathered together the sheets of paper.

'So, what is it?'

'This is a list of one hundred and seventy-three properties owned by the same company. They include both Violet's and Byron's property.'

Jemima let out a long whistle. 'That's a hell of a lot. There's some serious money behind that enterprise.'

'There sure is. But I can't see that it gets us anywhere.'

'Maybe not, but do you have details of the company?'

'Only the name and a PO box address.'

'Check them out with Companies House. It shouldn't take long, and at least we'll have the information should we need to go back to it at a later stage. Though at the moment, I can't imagine why we would.'

* * *

Jemima and Broadbent spoke to those members of the SOCO team who worked closely with Toombes. It immediately became apparent that he was disliked and mistrusted, but they didn't appear to think that Toombes had actually done anything wrong — he had just made them feel uncomfortable. They said he was good at his job and a reliable worker. As no official complaint had been made against him, there were no grounds on which he could be dismissed.

The interviews had been conducted in a small room overlooking the central administrative area where the SOCOs were based. From where Jemima was seated, she was aware that Toombes had remained at his workstation for the entire time. He was clearly aware of what they were doing, but appeared unconcerned. When they had finished, he even smiled and wished them both a pleasant evening as they headed for the exit.

The man made her skin crawl. Jemima glanced at her watch and cursed.

'What's up?' asked Broadbent.

'I arranged to meet Violet at her house. I should have been there thirty minutes ago.'

'Well, it's not as though she's in any immediate danger. Toombes has been at his desk all afternoon.'

'Yeah, you're right.'

'Do you want me to tag along?' Broadbent asked.

'No, get yourself home. It's nothing urgent. I'll bring you up to speed tomorrow once I've had a chance to check something out.'

CHAPTER 16

As Jemima pulled up outside Violet's house, the first thing she noticed was the artificial light that streamed from each of the windows. Wasting energy was one of her pet hates. Nick had a habit of leaving the lights on at home, and Jemima was fed up of having to go around switching them off.

Jemima rang the doorbell and waited, but there was no answer. She tried again and bent down to shout through the letterbox. Moments later, as she peered through the narrow opening, she saw Violet rush towards the door gripping a kitchen knife.

'Whoa! It's me, DS Huxley. Put the knife down and open the door!' Jemima shouted. She heard the knife clatter to the floor as the door was being unlocked. 'What's with the knife?'

'He threatened me,' sobbed Violet.

'Who threatened you?'

'Byron, of course, and it's your fault! You were late. I was here by myself, and he threatened me.' Violet's voice was unusually harsh and shrill, each word spilling out of her mouth in a rapid staccato as she battled to control her mounting hysteria.

It was clear to Jemima that Violet wasn't putting on a show. She really was terrified. She was noticeably pale and had clearly been crying. Her eyes were bloodshot and puffy.

'Violet, listen to me, Byron was at work. He's been there all afternoon. I saw him with my own eyes. He couldn't possibly have got here before me.'

'He rang me and told me that I'd never be safe.'

'He's got your mobile number?'

'He called the landline. If you don't believe me, then listen to what he said. I pressed record before I picked up. It's the proof you need to do something about him.'

'Let me hear it,' said Jemima, as she stepped into the narrow hallway. 'And put that knife away. You shouldn't be carrying it around. You could hurt yourself. Where's Lucy?'

'I didn't tell her I was coming here.'

'Why not? The reason for asking her was so that you wouldn't be alone in the house. If you'd listened to my advice, you wouldn't have gone through this by yourself.'

'Lucy and I have fallen out. Truth be told, I think she feels trapped having me stay with her. It's one thing seeing someone for a couple of hours every so often, but having them camp out in your personal space soon becomes unbearable.'

'Let me listen to the recording,' said Jemima. She was determined not to become embroiled in any discussion about her sibling. Their sisterly relationship was fragile at the best of times, and Jemima knew that if she made a comment that subsequently got back to Lucy, it had the potential to make future contact between them impossible.

Jemima sat down as Violet played the recording. The silence was shattered by the eerie sound of an electronically altered voice, which issued a chilling threat. *I'm with you, Violet. You can't escape me. I'll always be with you. Catch you later.*

It was like something out of a horror movie and Jemima could feel her heart racing, even though the threat wasn't aimed at her. No wonder Violet was terrified.

'Can you arrest him now?' begged Violet.

'I'm afraid it's not that simple.'

'It never is,' snapped Violet.

'The voice has been altered. Have you tried 1471 to see who made the call?'

'No, I didn't think of doing that.'

'I'll try it now,' said Jemima. She keyed in the four digits only to find that the caller had withheld their number. 'I'll take the machine back to the station and see if anyone can clean up the recording. If they can, we may be able to listen to the actual voice. You do realize that it's not safe for you to stay here?'

'I've got nowhere else to go.'

'Of course you have. Even if you don't want to go back to Lucy's, your grandparents will take you in.'

'But I don't wa—'

'Swallow your pride, Violet. You might not want to, but you must. You're clearly not safe here. Not with Byron living next door. Get your things together now while I'm here with you. I'll ring your grandfather and tell him that you're on your way.'

The unexpected turn of events meant that Jemima decided to delay a detailed search of Violet's house. The immediate priority now was to get Violet to her grandparents' house, where she would be safe. Once she had seen to that, Jemima would take the recording back to the station to see if it could be cleaned up.

When they eventually stepped outside, Jemima could see that Toombes's house was in darkness.

'I'll follow you to make sure you get there safely,' she said.

As Jemima was about to drive away, a car pulled up, and Byron Toombes got out.

'What's happened?' he asked.

Jemima was unable to tell whether the man was a good actor or genuinely had no knowledge of the phone call Violet had recently received.

'Where have you been, Mr Toombes?' asked Jemima.

'You know where I've been. I was at work. You saw me there,' he said.

'When we last spoke, I advised you to stay away from Violet, yet she has only just returned to her house, and has received a threatening phone call.'

'And you think that I made it?'

'Yes, I do,' said Jemima.

'I may be many things, but I'm not stupid. I've had no contact with Violet. I'm sorry she's had an upsetting phone call, but it wasn't me. I suggest you look elsewhere, because this is starting to feel like police harassment. You could find yourself in a lot of trouble if I make an official complaint.'

'I don't respond well to threats, Mr Toombes. So I'll ask you again, where were you in the last hour?'

'At work, and I can prove it. The security guard logged me out, so you'll be able to verify what I'm telling you. You can check the times I was active on my work computer-user profile. It'll even tell you which machine I used. But please, I'm begging you not to go down that route. You've already seen to it that my name is mud around there. It's not going to do much for my credibility if you start asking more questions. People are quick to jump to the wrong conclusion. You could ruin my career.'

'I'll have to check it out, as this incident appears to be linked to the previous allegation. Would you mind if I take a look inside your house and car?' asked Jemima. She knew that if he had been behind the phone call, there was a real possibility that he still had the phone and voice adaptor on him.

'Of course I mind. Why would I let you do that? I'm not a criminal. I've done nothing wrong.'

'If that's the case, why would you object? Surely you wouldn't have anything to hide? And it could help clear things up immediately.'

'I said no. It's an invasion of my privacy. If you want access to my house or car, you'll have to come back with a warrant. Until then, we're done,' Toombes snapped.

The conversation ended abruptly, as Toombes headed towards his house, opened the front door, stepped inside and shut it firmly behind him.

Jemima knew that she wasn't guaranteed to get a warrant to search Toombes's house or car. Even if one was granted, they might not find the evidence they needed to bring about a prosecution. Jemima's instinct told her that Toombes was responsible for making the intimidating phone call, but thinking something and being able to prove it were two very different things. Especially when dealing with someone intelligent enough to ensure that he had covered his tracks.

CHAPTER 17

Before entering the police station, Jemima scrolled through the contact list on her phone and selected a number. Yvette De Sousa picked up. Jemima explained what had just happened to Violet and asked if it would be possible to search the SOCO office that evening.

'I don't think you have reasonable grounds for searching the premises, but I'm happy to meet you there in about an hour, and you can watch me undertake a search. To cover myself, I'll have to search more than just Toombes's workstation and the area he usually frequents. So you'll need to set aside a few hours if we're going to make this look like a genuine search.'

Jemima didn't care how long it took. She agreed, and then left her car and headed into the police station. As there was no one on duty with the skills to attempt to clean up the electronically altered voice, she locked the device away for safekeeping.

* * *

When Jemima arrived at the SOCO building, she found that Yvette was already there.

'I'm delighted you agreed to this,' said Jemima.

'If your request had been about any other member of staff, my answer may very well have been different. But I know what Byron is capable of, and I want him gone. He's a danger to women and I don't want him as part of this team. Hopefully, we'll find something to incriminating, then I'll be able to get rid of him.'

The two women spent the best part of three hours conducting a thorough search of the building. Yvette checked the logs and CCTV for the time in question. There was a period when Toombes had strayed from his desk, but it appeared that he had been in the men's restroom throughout the duration. They found nothing to show that he had hidden a phone or a voice-altering device. As there was no CCTV in the vicinity of the toilets, it was impossible to know whether that was the location he had used to make the call.

Jemima and Yvette were both disappointed that they hadn't been able to find anything to tie Toombes to the phone call. Worse still, they failed to uncover any evidence to suggest that he was up to no good.

'We can't carry on like this,' said Yvette. 'First thing in the morning I'm going to contact Toombes and tell him that he's suspended. I know we haven't found any definitive proof that he made that phone call, but I can't risk him compromising any crime scenes. We both know what he's capable of, and I'm not going to allow him to drag this department into disrepute. I should have taken the initiative and acted sooner. Instead, I've been reluctant to act because I've put my sister's feelings first, but that stops now. I'll just have to face any potential consequences if he challenges my decision.'

* * *

Kennedy was still at his desk when Jemima returned to the station later that evening.

'What are you doing here so late in the day?' he asked.

Jemima filled him in on the recent developments. She was worried about Violet, especially after hearing the sinister voice recording. Toombes was such a dislikeable character, and Jemima didn't trust him. He was intelligent enough to know how to play the game and was more than capable of staying one step ahead of them. He was cunning enough to come across as being reasonable and misunderstood, but Jemima was convinced that there was a dark side to him. She wanted to shake things up to get Toombes to show his hand, but she needed Kennedy's backing before taking things further.

'Tread carefully, Huxley. You're wandering through a minefield. At the moment we've no proof he's actually committed a crime. It's just speculation on our part. On the other hand, we're the only line of defence that Violet has. So whichever way you intend to play this, keep in mind that if you push Toombes too far, it could have serious implications for her.'

'I appreciate that, but Toombes needs to know that we're going to keep an eye on him. It may even be sufficient to make him back off. Make him realize that if he continues with his fixation, there will be consequences for him. At the moment he seems to think he's untouchable. It'd be good to give him a taste of reality.'

'Fair enough,' Kennedy replied. 'From what you've told me, it's unlikely that Toombes is going to leave Violet alone. And things could escalate if we do nothing. The last thing any of us want is for him to go full-on psycho-stalker. Violet could end up seriously injured or dead.'

'My thoughts exactly,' said Jemima. 'I'm going to request a log of activity on Toombes's mobile phone. But I also want to get a search warrant for his home and vehicle. Yvette De Sousa told me that she's suspending him first thing tomorrow. Ideally, I'd like to hit him with the search at five o'clock tomorrow morning. It'll throw him off balance.'

'Fine, I'll arrange for the warrant. You sort out a team. On a different note, how are things between you and Broadbent now?' asked Kennedy.

'As far as I can tell, he's finally starting to accept the situation. There's a definite thaw in hostilities and moments when we actually seem to be working well together. I'd say things are moving in the right direction.'

CHAPTER 18

When the alarm went off at half-past three the next morning, it caught Jemima by surprise. She'd been deeply asleep and bolted upright, heart pounding. She'd barely managed four hours sleep, as she'd been so wired.

'Switch it off, Jem!' moaned Nick, turning on to his side and diving even further beneath the duvet.

Her husband's sleepy protestation brought Jemima to her senses. She reached out, hit the off-switch and swung her legs out of bed, feeling sick with exhaustion.

Time was not on her side. Making arrangements for the search so late in the day had not allowed time to brief any of the search team, and as she needed to ensure that everyone knew what they were supposed to do, it was imperative to get to the station as soon as possible.

Feeling dog-tired and urgently needing to wake herself up, she headed downstairs to brew a pot of strong coffee. After switching the machine on, her next stop was a shower. She kept the water as cold as possible. It was an unpleasant but effective experience. At 4.10 a.m. Jemima shut the front door behind her, feeling a whole lot more alert and energized than she had forty minutes earlier.

An advantage of starting so early in the day was that there was barely any traffic on the road. Ten minutes later, Jemima was parking in the secure area at the rear of the station. She locked the car and headed towards the entrance.

Apart from Jemima and Broadbent, there were five other officers taking part in the search. One of them would be tasked with keeping a close eye on Toombes, and as soon as she finished the briefing, they were ready to go.

'Open up, Mr Toombes! We've a warrant to search your home and vehicle.' Jemima's index finger remained on the doorbell as she repeatedly pounded the door with her free hand.

The majority of people would still be in bed at that time in the morning. With the racket Jemima was making, she would undoubtedly wake many of the street's other residents. She experienced a moment of guilt about waking so many people at such an early hour. But knowing that many of them would take an interest in what was happening helped justify the disturbance. They'd realize that Toombes was being investigated by the police, which in turn, would ensure that more people kept an eye on him. It should ultimately make it harder for Toombes to step out of line in future.

'Any sign of life?' she asked, directing the question at Broadbent.

He was studying the windows to see if a light was switched on. 'Nothing. He's probably trying to pretend he's not there.'

'His car's here, and as far as he's concerned, he's going into work in a few hours. He's definitely inside. Break it down,' ordered Jemima, stepping back to allow access to the officer holding a battering ram.

There was a dull thud accompanied by the sound of splintering wood, and the door separated from the frame.

'What the fuck are you doing? You'll pay for the damage you've caused,' yelled Toombes, as he ran down the stairs. He was in his boxers and a T-shirt. His hair was sticking up at odd angles, and one side of his face was redder than the other. He'd clearly been asleep.

'We've got a warrant to conduct a search of this property and of your vehicle,' said Jemima. 'We also have authorization to confiscate all communication devices at this time. Everything will be returned to you at a later stage.'

'You've gotta be kidding. This is persecution, and I'm sick of it.'

'You've been told on numerous occasions to stay away from Violet Watkins, but you've continued to harass her,' said Jemima.

'You've no proof, or else you'd arrest me.'

'We'll see what this search throws up. First of all, I want your car keys and mobile phone,' said Jemima. She held out a hand, repeatedly clicking her fingers to emphasize the fact that she had no intention of being kept waiting.

'Get them yourself. They're on the kitchen table,' said Toombes.

A uniformed officer headed towards the kitchen and returned with the items.

'Bag the phone, then you and Bradbury can search his car,' said Jemima.

'You're not taking my phone,' snapped Toombes.

'We are. We'll also be removing any PCs or laptops we find. Now sit down and stay out of our way. If you make any attempt to interfere with this search, you will be arrested.'

Jemima was delighted that they had caught Toombes off guard. On this occasion, he was unable to muster the smug, superior expression they were accustomed to seeing. Instead, he looked angry. It felt good to rattle his confidence and finally get him on the back foot.

'I'll get some clothes for you to put on,' Jemima said, addressing Toombes. She turned back to her team. 'Keep a close eye on him. If he moves, I want to know about it.'

'I haven't been anywhere near Violet since she first reported me,' Toombes protested. 'The woman's either delusional or someone else is targeting her. But whatever it is, leave me out of it. It's got nothing to do with me. I'm the real victim here. Someone's setting me up.'

Jemima ignored Toombes's assertions of innocence. There was no doubt in her mind that he was guilty. She just needed the evidence to prove it. 'Broadbent, you and Davies take the downstairs and the garden shed. Rowlands, you're upstairs with me.'

'You'd better be careful with my stuff!' yelled Toombes. 'You owe me for that door. If you break anything, you'll pay for it.'

Jemima ignored him and focused on the task in hand. This was their one and only chance to scrutinize Toombes's home environment.

Jemima headed to the main bedroom and hurriedly selected some clothes for Toombes to put on. She took them downstairs and ordered him to get dressed. When he asked if he could have some privacy, she refused. Toombes glowered but said nothing.

As Jemima returned and began to work her way through the upstairs rooms, she noted how meticulous Toombes was. Everything was scrupulously clean and tidy. There was no dust, clutter or even a sign that anything was out of place. It crossed her mind that if she could only get Nick to take a similar approach, their own domestic space would become much more appealing.

It was apparent that Toombes favoured a minimalist approach to life. He appeared to be fanatical about hygiene, which was probably exacerbated by situations he encountered while at work. Jemima had already noted that there were no carpets anywhere in the house. The only exception was in the main bedroom, where a small rug covered a section of floorboards. Her first thought was to ignore it and move on, as it seemed a logical assumption that Toombes would have placed the rug there as he didn't want to get out of bed and step directly on to the wood. But as she continued to work her way through his possessions, the rug began to bother her.

Jemima bent down, picked up the rug and placed it on the bed. She studied the newly uncovered section of floor. At first sight, it appeared exactly the same as the rest of the area, but the more she thought about it, the more convinced she was that Toombes had placed the rug there for a specific reason.

The smell of wood polish became more noticeable as she dropped to her hands and knees to take a closer look. Jemima ran her hands over the boards. They were perfectly smooth and cool to the touch. She was about to replace the rug when she spotted something strange. It wasn't obvious unless you were looking for it, but one of the boards was far shorter than any of the others. In fact, it was no more than a couple of feet in length, which was odd, given the fact that it was in a central location. Getting back down on all fours, she examined the floor more closely. Scanning the boards, she noticed that they were nailed to the joists, but this small section had nothing holding it in place.

Jemima reached out and pressed down on the nearest edge of the board. It moved slightly. Lowering her face even further, she spotted a small indent on the side of the board. It was barely noticeable and could easily have passed as a fault in the wood, but Jemima knew that Toombes wasn't the sort of person to tolerate imperfections.

Jemima jumped to her feet and headed downstairs to find Broadbent. 'I need to speak to you outside,' she said in a hushed tone, so that Toombes couldn't hear what she was saying.

Broadbent went into the recently searched garden shed and selected a small flathead screwdriver that was lying on a workbench. Without saying another word, they both returned to the house and headed upstairs.

Within seconds the small section of floorboard was lifted to reveal a laptop, various SIM cards and numerous memory sticks, along with a stash of pornographic material. They would have to take everything back to the police station to establish whether or not these items linked Toombes to the campaign against Violet, but at the moment they were sufficient to take him in for questioning.

'Well done, guv,' said Broadbent, tapping her on the back.

It was the first time he'd ever praised her, and Jemima could tell that his admiration was genuine. Those three little words gave her a warm glow. It seemed as though her persistence had paid off.

'This isn't just down to me. It was a team effort,' Jemima said. 'Now let's bag this lot up then go downstairs and arrest the bastard.'

Jemima allowed Broadbent to go ahead of her as they headed downstairs. Having completed their searches, the other officers were gathered around Toombes. Their restrained hostility towards him was palpable.

As Broadbent emerged from the hallway, six pairs of eyes stared expectantly in his direction. He held the evidence bag aloft and smiled.

'The honour's all yours, Dan,' said Jemima. She would have loved to have arrested Toombes herself, but she was prepared to be magnanimous. It was a gesture she knew would be appreciated.

The moment he realized that they'd discovered his hiding place, Toombes's complexion paled. There was an undeniable expression of fear on his face as Broadbent read him his rights. It was all the confirmation Jemima needed. She knew that whatever they had found would be enough to incriminate the man. His luck had finally run out.

Toombes hung his head in defeat.

'You don't need to cuff me. I'll come quietly,' he muttered.

'It's your call.' Broadbent turned to Jemima.

'We don't do requests. You've been arrested, so you'll be cuffed,' Jemima told Toombes.

'Shall we take the evidence in our car?' asked one of the officers.

'No, Broadbent can hold on to it,' said Jemima. She knew the likely importance of this evidence and had no intention of letting it out of her sight. 'Let's get you to the station,' she said, grabbing Toombes's arm. She marched him out to the car, opened the rear door, placed her hand on the top of his head and pushed him into the vehicle.

* * *

Jemima and Broadbent headed back to the police station in silence. For once, they were keen to talk to each other, but they both knew better than to say anything in front of Toombes. There would be plenty of time for sharing their excitement.

As usual, Jemima had chosen to drive, and for once she was sticking to the speed limit. Broadbent was in the passenger seat, with the evidence bag in the footwell, held securely in place between his legs.

As they made their way towards the city centre, the traffic steadily increased. It was particularly busy as they approached a major junction controlled by lights. The light turned red, and they were third in the queue. As it turned green, the cars ahead moved forward, and Jemima followed as they still had the right of way.

They were mid-junction when they were rammed side-on. Tyres squealed as their vehicle was forced in a direction it wasn't meant to go. They were trapped, helpless, as the car was shunted, airbags deployed, and they almost flipped.

Everything happened so fast. Broadbent's door buckled inwards as a side airbag hit his leg. There was the sickening sound of metal against metal as panels ripped open like a flimsy tin can. Another airbag exploded out of the steering wheel, hitting Jemima forcefully in the face. A searing pain shot up her hand and wrist as the steering wheel lurched precariously close to her chest.

She tried to regain control, but the airbag was suffocating her. Everything went black.

CHAPTER 19

Somewhere in the distance, Broadbent was shouting. As Jemima struggled to open her eyes, it felt as though she had the hangover from hell. At first, she had no idea where she was or what had happened. She felt something touch then shake her left shoulder. As she came to her senses, she realized that Broadbent was trying to attract her attention. She looked at him, perplexed, not knowing what had happened.

'We've crashed.' His voice seemed far away, as though it was coming from underwater.

'Wh—' She struggled to make sense of what he was saying, but her ears were ringing, and she was in pain.

'We've crashed! I can't open my door. Toombes has gone. Someone let him out. He grabbed your keys, so he'll be able to ditch the cuffs. You were out of it, and I couldn't do anything to stop him.'

As Jemima turned to stare at him, Broadbent's words suddenly began to make sense. 'Have you still got the evidence bag?' she asked.

'Yes. Toombes couldn't reach it. If he'd been able to open my door, it would have been a different matter.'

* * *

It took the best part of an hour for Jemima and Broadbent to be freed from the vehicle. In the meantime, another officer came to collect the evidence and take it back to the station, so they could still continue to build a case against Toombes while they were searching for him. They were taken to the hospital for checks, but luckily neither of them had suffered severe injuries and they were able to get back to work.

It was approaching lunchtime when they arrived back at the station. Despite her injuries, Jemima managed a smile as they both walked into the incident room and were mobbed by concerned colleagues. It seemed that the accident had somehow made her one of them. She had barely had time to sit down before someone placed a mug of coffee on her desk. She must have looked at it a bit suspiciously, as the officer who had put it there wished her well and reassured her it was safe to drink.

'Good to see you both,' said Kennedy, striding into the room. 'I think it's safe to say that they've finally accepted you as one of us, Huxley. It's just a shame that a squad car had to be written off for these reprobates to finally come around to my way of thinking. But they've always been a hard lot to win over.' At the sound of laughter and chatter, Kennedy turned his attention back to the others in the room. 'Come on, that's enough. It's time you lot got back to work. Every second wasted gives Toombes more chance to go to ground.'

'Did you find anything useful?' asked Jemima.

'His laptop is password protected. I've got the tech team looking at things as we speak. Hopefully, we'll hear back from them soon.'

'What about the USB sticks?'

'I'm afraid they're encrypted too. On the face of it, it seems Toombes has got something to hide. As frustrating as it is, we've just got to be patient and give the techies time to work their magic.'

'Any leads on his location?' asked Jemima.

'Not so far. We've CCTV footage of Toombes making his escape. Once he'd nabbed your keys, he somehow managed to persuade a young lad to release the cuffs. God only knows how he managed to pull that off, but he did. He's dropped off the radar as he's clearly familiar with the location of surveillance cameras. But I've circulated his description, and we've got officers out looking for him.'

'Any chance we were rammed on purpose?' asked Broadbent.

'It was my first thought, but no. The other driver tested positive for alcohol and cocaine. She was off her face.'

* * *

It was approaching early evening when Jemima's phone rang. Having only just decided to call it a day, both she and Broadbent were aware that a phone call at this time was unlikely to be good news.

Jemima listened in silence as the person on the other end of the line relayed the information. What she was told was so unexpected that she reached blindly for the chair and slumped into it.

'We're on our way,' she said. 'The granddaughter knows us, and if Toombes is with her, then we're best placed to deal with it. I want the property secured. No one's to enter it until we get there. Get hold of Yvette De Sousa as a priority. Tell her that no SOCO directly connected with Toombes is to attend the scene. We can't risk evidence being compromised. And the same goes for the SOCOs. They're not to go in until I say so.' Jemima ended the call and looked up to meet Broadbent's gaze.

'What's happened?' he asked.

'We've got to go,' she said, hurriedly wiping away a telltale sign of emotion. She stood up and grabbed a set of car keys. 'Judge Pickering's just reported an incident at his house. He arrived home to find his wife murdered. It's possible that Violet's still inside the house.'

CHAPTER 20

When Jemima and Broadbent reached Judge Pickering's house, Jemima noted that uniformed officers were already in attendance at the scene. 'I take it that no one has gone in or out of the property?'

'No. The owner was in a right state when we got here. He was sat on the step outside the front door.'

From the corner of her eye, Jemima spotted some movement coming from the rear of an ambulance. As she headed towards the vehicle, she spotted Judge Pickering being attended to by a couple of paramedics. He looked bewildered, old and bereft. It was difficult to reconcile him with the sharp-minded man who ruled over his courtroom with a rod of iron.

As Jemima approached, he glanced up, and she noticed a hint of recognition in his face. 'She's dead. My wife's dead,' he mumbled.

'Come on, sir. We should get you into the ambulance. You need to have a doctor take a look at you,' said the younger of the paramedics, as he helped him into the vehicle.

Pickering shuffled forward compliantly — head bowed, barely capable of putting one foot in front of the other.

'What about Violet? Is she inside the house?' Jemima asked.

'I don't know . . . possibly . . . I think so,' replied Pickering.

'Arrange for another ambulance crew to attend. It's possible his granddaughter is still inside and could be seriously injured,' said Jemima. She ran towards the front of the house and spoke to the officer on guard. 'Broadbent and I are going inside. Don't let anyone else in or out until I give the all-clear.'

The officer nodded.

'I've got us both a set of shoe coverings,' said Broadbent.

'Violet could still be in there. Are you OK about going inside? It could be gruesome. You're not queasy, are you?' asked Jemima, as she bent down to slip the coverings over her shoes.

'Why? What have you heard?' he asked. The prickly tone of his voice sounded a little too defensive.

As they made their way through the hallway, there was no apparent sign that anything was wrong. A radio played in a room up ahead. The classical music was loud, and Jemima knew it would have helped to mask the sound of any potential intruder.

They entered the kitchen to find Cynthia Pickering's body slumped forward on a kitchen chair. A cursory glance told Jemima that the woman had been reading a magazine at the kitchen table when her attacker had approached from behind. A freshly baked pie was cooling on a rack placed on the granite work surface. The murder weapon — a rolling pin — lay discarded on the floor. The few floury remains of pastry upon its wooden surface were mixed with blood, bone and brain matter.

Jemima had investigated many violent crimes, but racking up the numbers didn't lessen the impact it had on her. Some officers, mainly men, claimed to have become desensitized to certain situations, but Jemima thought it was just macho bullshit. She swore to herself that if she ever reached a point in her career when she became blasé about the awfulness of what she was seeing, it would be time for her to walk away from the force.

Jemima had no intention of moving further into the room. She had seen all she needed to see. From the neck up, Cynthia Pickering was unrecognizable, such had been the force of the blows to her skull.

To the rear of the kitchen, the patio doors were fully open, each held securely in place by a terracotta plant pot. As Cynthia's back was to this, Jemima was confident that it was the way the intruder had entered the property.

As there was no sign of Violet, they methodically searched the downstairs rooms. When they found each of them empty, they headed upstairs. Jemima took the lead.

Everything appeared undisturbed and ordinary in each of the rooms on the upper floor, until they came across a door they were unable to open. As it wasn't lockable with a key, it was apparent that someone had barricaded it shut.

'Violet, its Jemima, Lucy's sister!' she shouted.

When there was no response, Jemima pressed her ear to the door, listening for any sound from inside the room. Hearing nothing, Jemima weighed up the possibilities. If Violet was inside the room, she was either dead, unconscious, or she was in there with the killer. It was also possible, but far less likely, that the killer was alone inside and had barricaded the door.

Jemima took out her phone and dialled Violet's mobile number. Within seconds a ringtone sounded on the other side of the door. The call remained unanswered, but at least they knew that Violet was probably in the room.

'We've got to get that door open,' said Jemima.

'What do you expect me to do about it?' asked Broadbent.

'Force it open, or break the bloody thing down, that's what!' snapped Jemima.

'So I'm just the hired muscle?' asked Broadbent. He made no attempt to hide his contempt.

'For fuck's sake, Broadbent, this isn't the time or the place for you to have a hissy fit. Violet's life could be in danger. So just break the bloody door down!' Jemima turned back to the door. 'Violet, are you all right in there? The paramedics will be here soon. We need to get inside so that we can help you. But we can't seem to open the door. Talk to me, Violet. Or make some sort of noise. I need to know whether you're all right.'

There was still no response.

Broadbent put his weight against the door. It moved slightly, but not far enough to allow them to see inside, let alone enter the room. 'How about you giving me a hand?' he said. His face was red and glistening with sweat.

'Looks as though you need to work on your fitness level,' said Jemima. 'Come on, shift over and let me help get this door open.' She realized quickly that it would be a painful procedure, as the injury to her hand and wrist that morning was still sore.

With their combined efforts, the door inched open, and it soon became apparent that some heavy furniture had been placed against it to barricade it shut.

'Won't be long now,' puffed Broadbent.

As soon as the gap was wide enough, Jemima squeezed through it. She found Violet, naked and unconscious, on the floor. Fearing the worst, she rushed over and felt for a pulse. She held her breath as she tried to locate it and sighed with relief when she found one.

'She's alive, but in a bad way. Get the paramedics up here now,' shouted Jemima.

Broadbent raced down the stairs.

Jemima quickly assessed the scene, committing everything to memory. Violet had a nasty head injury and fresh bruising on her inner thighs. It suggested that the young woman had been knocked unconscious then raped.

Although it was a crime scene, Jemima pulled the duvet from the bed and draped it over Violet. She couldn't stand the thought that anyone should see the young woman in such an undignified and vulnerable state.

As the duvet touched her skin, Violet opened her eyes and stared blankly. She had no idea what was going on.

'Try to relax,' said Jemima. 'I'm not going to hurt you. I'm just covering you up to make you a little warmer. You've had a knock to the head. By the look of it, you've lost a lot of blood. The paramedics will be here soon.' As she uttered the flimsy reassurance, there was the sound of footsteps on the stairs, and a female paramedic appeared in the room.

'Let me take a look,' the paramedic said. 'OK, sweetheart, I'm going to have to get a line into you. You'll feel a sharp prick, but I promise I'll be as gentle as I can.' She turned to her colleague. 'We'll need the stretcher. She's not in a fit state to make it out of here under her own steam.' Turning her attention back to Violet, the woman continued to work quickly. 'We'll take you to the hospital soon, sweetheart. Now I want you to keep your head still, and follow my finger with your eyes.'

Violet failed to respond.

Jemima stared down at the scene and the breath caught in her throat. There was no doubt in her mind that Byron Toombes was responsible for everything that had gone on inside this house. She had known all along that Toombes was capable of hurting Violet, but she had failed to stop it from happening. As a result, Violet had been raped, and her grandmother had lost her life in a brutal attack.

Jemima had failed and would have to learn to live with the guilt. It was of no consolation that she had done everything within the confines of the law to stop him.

CHAPTER 21

The evening sun was low and bright as Jemima emerged from the house. It was dazzling, and she squinted until her eyes adjusted. As Jemima looked out across the immediate area, she saw that the SOCO team had arrived. It was an anxious few minutes until she reassured herself that they were not Toombes's colleagues.

'That's the SIO,' said Broadbent, pointing Jemima out to the lead SOCO.

'You should have waited until we arrived. You could have compromised the scene,' said the man. He was significantly taller and older than Jemima and had a hard edge to his voice. The clipped speech emphasized his officious manner. It was as though he was reprimanding a junior instead of taking a collaborative approach with the officer in charge.

'It wasn't an option,' Jemima told him. 'We took every available precaution to preserve evidence. There was another victim in the house, who needs immediate medical attention. If we hadn't gone in when we did, there might very well have been another fatality.' Jemima hated the fact that she felt compelled to explain herself. It was demeaning. She was sure that he wouldn't have spoken to a male officer in such a manner, but this was hardly the time or place to make a stand. Instead, she made the decision to rise above it, as she needed his cooperation to get things processed as quickly and thoroughly as possible. 'Shall I walk you through the scene?'

'It would be appreciated,' he replied. It was noticeable that his tone had softened, presumably because Jemima had passed whatever strange test it was the man had set.

'There's a single fatality in the kitchen,' said Jemima. 'I believe she was murdered with a rolling pin. The rear French doors are open, and the victim was sat with her back to them. That's how I believe the killer accessed the property. The murder weapon suggests to me that the killer didn't set out with the intention of killing anyone. It was a case of the victim being in the wrong place at the wrong time, forcing him to improvise and use whatever was available.

'I believe the real reason for him entering the property was the second victim, a young woman who as far as I could tell, was attacked then raped in an upstairs room. I also believe that the perpetrator could be a SOCO named—'

'Byron Toombes,' said the man, jumping in to finish Jemima's sentence.

'Has Yvette De Sousa explained why a different SOCO team needed to work the crime scene?'

'Yes, I am aware of the background. It's the reason we took so long to arrive. We usually work away from the area and so had further to travel. You have no need to worry. We don't know Toombes. We'll process the scene as we would any other.'

'I'd expect nothing less,' said Jemima. 'As well as my partner and I, two paramedics entered the property and went upstairs to treat and remove the second victim. The husband entered the house, presumably by the front door and discovered his wife's body in the kitchen. As you would expect, he was in a state of shock. I have no idea if he touched anything or compromised the murder scene in any way.'

Jemima emerged from the property once more to find Broadbent talking to someone on his mobile. He ended the call and turned to her.

'While I was out here, I took a look around,' he said. 'I spotted the CCTV cameras at the end of the road. I also noticed that some of the properties have cameras fixed to the walls as part of their home-security systems, which is hardly surprising as this is a wealthy neighbourhood.'

'Excellent thought,' said Jemima. She noticed the way Broadbent stood a little bit taller, buoyed by the encouragement. It made her appreciate how the odd kind word here or there could boost his confidence.

'I've just been in touch with the station and asked them to get someone to obtain the footage,' Broadbent continued. 'Oh, and Kennedy's on his way. He's managed to drum up a couple more plods to go house to house. They'll be briefed to request access to any home-security footage of the area.'

There was the sound of approaching vehicles. Moments later, Kennedy appeared.

'Nasty business, this,' he said, shaking his head in disbelief. 'I'll coordinate things at this end, Huxley. You and Broadbent get yourselves back to the station. You've both had a hell of a day so far. I want you both to focus your attention on Toombes. This incident may or may not be down to him. Until that's determined, I intend to keep an open mind about the perpetrator. Let's face it, people in Pickering's profession make a fair few enemies.

'Shortly before I left the station, the techies sent word that they were close to cracking Toombes's passwords. Hopefully, by the time you get back there, you'll be able to take a look at things.'

'What about Violet?' asked Jemima.

'You can still take the lead on Violet, but as I understand it, she's going nowhere at the moment. I've sent an officer to the hospital to stand guard, just in case whoever attacked her plans to have another go. I've been told categorically that you won't be allowed to speak with her until tomorrow morning.'

CHAPTER 22

Any thoughts of finishing at a reasonable time were out of the window. Back at the station, Jemima rummaged in her purse and gave Broadbent a twenty-pound note.

'It's going to be a late one, so grab us a selection of things from the canteen. Get whatever you want for yourself. I'd like a chicken sandwich and a coffee. We're going to need something to keep us going.'

Twenty minutes later, Broadbent returned to the incident room laden with supplies.

Jemima was staring intently at the monitor of a stan-dalone machine.

'What're you looking at?' he asked, as he placed everything on the desk and took the mug of coffee over to Jemima.

'It's a spreadsheet. Toombes has named the file with a random mixture of numbers and characters, so it's not obvious what it relates to. The techies have only been able to access this first sheet. It's clear from the entries that they are linked to numerous hidden protected sheets. I've a hunch it's some sort of financial document. If you look across the rows, the entries are often repeated with occasional gaps. When the entries recommence, the number in that row has increased.'

'That sort of stuff's way over my head,' said Broadbent.

'Could he be blackmailing people? Or providing some sort of service?' asked Jemima.

'Shit!' spluttered Broadbent, as he struggled to swallow the food he was chewing. 'It's possible he could be disposing of or contaminating evidence from crime scenes in return for regular payments.'

'If that's the case, then the force really is in trouble. He's been a SOCO for more than a decade. He could have worked thousands of crime scenes,' said Jemima. The theory seemed somewhat far-fetched, but Toombes was in a position to do such a thing. And it wasn't as if the man had a moral compass. The scenario was too awful to contemplate.

Before they had a chance to discuss things further, Aled Quinn — one of the force's technical team — came trotting into the room. 'You should take a look at this,' he said, holding out a memory stick.

Jemima felt her heart miss a beat. 'What's on it?' she asked.

'He's filmed people, but not in a homemade movie sense. This contains footage from inside a property. I'm talking about weeks', even months' worth of footage. And I don't think the person knew they were being filmed. I've watched some of it, and it seems as though there were surveillance cameras located in different parts of the property. It's not just visual. There's sound too. He's been listening in and watching everything that's been going on inside that house.'

'Let me take a look,' said Jemima, as she stood up to allow Aled to access the machine.

The hardware for day-to-day use was not the most up-to-date. This was one of those moments that took the feeling of frustration to a whole new level.

'Almost there,' reassured Aled, drumming his fingers on the desktop.

As the file loaded, Jemima gasped for air. She was so caught up in the moment that she hadn't realized she had been holding her breath.

'So the dirty bastard's been spying on Violet,' said Broadbent.

Jemima and Broadbent both moved closer to the screen as the film began to play. 'But that's not Violet or her house,' muttered Jemima. 'So who the hell is that woman stepping out of the shower?'

'And where the fuck is that property, because it's not Toombes's house either?' said Broadbent.

'You're right, it's not,' said Jemima.

'Could he have bought the footage off someone else?' suggested Aled.

'I don't know, but there's something we need to check out at Violet's house. You're driving, Dan.' Jemima tossed him the set of car keys as she grabbed her coffee and sandwich.

* * *

'Why are we going to Violet's house? How are we going to get in?' asked Broadbent as he negotiated the traffic.

'I want to check out something one of her colleagues said to me. As for how we are going to get in . . . well, don't ask,' said Jemima.

When Broadbent eventually stopped the car outside Violet's house, Jemima gulped down the final swig of coffee.

'Perfect timing,' she said. 'Now I suggest you look the other way if you value your career. At least that way you can deny all knowledge of alleged wrongdoing.'

'Christ! You're going to pick the lock, aren't you?'

'Shh!' hissed Jemima. 'Keep your voice down. I don't want the neighbours to get wind of what I'm about to do.'

'And there was me thinking you were a right goody two shoes. How wrong was I?' Broadbent shook his head in admiration and gave a smile of approval.

'Believe me, Dan, you haven't scratched the surface with me yet,' said Jemima. She quickly rummaged through her bag, extracted two small pieces of metal, inserted them in the lock and set about opening the door. It was a technique she'd mastered from studying YouTube videos — that, together with hours of practice.

'You'll be telling me next that you're a cat burglar in your spare time.'

'Not quite, but it's a handy skill to have if you ever find yourself locked out.'

'What's so important that you need to get in here tonight?'

'I think Toombes might have bugged the property. If my hunch is correct, there'll be at least two cameras — one in the lounge and another in the main bedroom. Though having seen that recording, there's likely to be others located throughout the house.'

'If you were going to have hidden cameras, I can understand that the bedroom would be a favoured spot. But what makes you think there's one in the lounge?'

'One of Violet's colleagues told me that something caught her eye on the wallpaper. She recalled that it was towards the centre of one of the flowers. She was about to take a closer look at it when Toombes came along and spilled a glass of wine down her. He claimed it was accidental, but I think he could have done it on purpose to distract her. The tactic obviously worked. She told me she was so focused on removing the stain that she forgot all about it until I asked her if Toombes had behaved oddly.'

'You could be on to something. Do you know which wall she was referring to?'

'No idea. I suggest that you take those two and I'll take these. It's probably best to just run our hands over the surface. If there's a camera embedded in there, we should be able to feel it. But we should put gloves on first, so as not to destroy any potential evidence.'

It took less than five minutes to locate the device.

'What do we do now?' asked Broadbent.

'Nothing, we lock up and keep schtum until I've had a chance to speak to Violet. If she gives us permission to undertake a search, then the evidence won't be compromised. A few hours' delay won't make any difference. We just need to play the game.

'I'm going to put in a request for an officer to be posted outside both of these properties. I think there's little chance Toombes would risk returning. He wouldn't want to get caught. But if I flag it up as a possibility, at least we'll know for certain that he wouldn't be able to access Violet's house and remove the spyware.'

'You're quite devious,' said Broadbent.

'I just do my best to read people and anticipate their actions. That way, we stand a chance of stacking the odds in our favour.'

CHAPTER 23

Early the next morning, Jemima was informed that they could interview Violet. It had taken a great deal of persistence and persuasion on her part to get the hospital staff to agree to it.

Back at the station, the tech team had worked through the night. They had succeeded in unlocking files from thirty-five of the fifty-eight USB sticks recovered from Toombes's house. The contents turned out to be more of the same surveillance footage from various unknown properties. The one thing they had in common was that young women had been targeted. It appeared that Toombes didn't have a particular preference when it came to type. He'd been content to indulge his voyeuristic fetish on whichever young woman was available.

Jemima had spoken to Yvette De Sousa, asking her to compile a list of every domestic crime scene Toombes had attended. It was unclear where and how he had managed to gain access to so many properties, but there was a possibility that he could have somehow used his position as a SOCO to enable him to install illegal surveillance equipment.

Yvette had asked for reassurances that the police wouldn't leak the theory to the press. Jemima convinced her that it was in no one's interest to do that. At the moment, it was just a line of enquiry that needed following up. None of the surveillance tapes might have been linked to his work as a SOCO. If that turned out to be the case, then leaking unfounded allegations would cause unnecessary and extensive damage to the credibility of the police force. It would also cast doubt on the credibility of evidence gathered by the SOCO team.

Jemima and Broadbent sat in silence as they travelled to the hospital. It wasn't that they had fallen out with each other — far from it. They were more united now than they had ever been. They were just lost in their own thoughts about how to approach their individual tasks.

It had been agreed that Jemima would interview Violet as she had already formed a relationship with her. And, given the nature of the attack, it seemed logical that Violet would be more forthcoming to another woman.

They had heard that Judge Pickering had been kept in hospital overnight. The shock of seeing his wife murdered in such a brutal fashion had affected him severely, and the doctors were running tests, as he had a heart condition. Jemima suggested that Broadbent spoke to the judge, though she thought that Pickering was unlikely to reveal any useful information.

'We'll meet back here when we've finished,' said Jemima. They had reached an intersection that would send them off in different directions to get to the respective wards.

Jemima disliked the smell of hospitals. The overpowering scent of industrial-strength disinfectant was so strong that you could almost taste it. She arrived on the ward as the medical team was walking away from Violet's bedside. Jemima could see that the young woman was awake. The nurse informed her that she could speak to Violet, but insisted that the conversation be brief, as her patient needed to rest.

As Jemima approached the bed, she noticed that a section of Violet's hair had been shaved to allow stitches to close a wound on her scalp. 'How're you feeling?' she asked.

'Awful,' replied Violet. Her voice was croaky.

'I appreciate this is a difficult time, but I need answers to some questions. Let me know if it's getting too much for you. But the sooner you tell me what happened, the sooner we can begin to find the person responsible,' said Jemima.

Violet's eyes had a faraway look, and tears trickled down her cheeks as she spoke. It was apparent that recalling the traumatic events was causing her to relive the fear and helplessness experienced at the time. 'It was B-Byron. I thought I'd be safe in my g-grandparents' house, but I wasn't. He attacked me when I c-came out of the shower. He must've been s-standing there, watching me. They told me that he r-raped me.'

'I'm so sorry, Violet,' said Jemima, reaching out to take her hand and squeezing it gently.

Violet took a deep, shuddering breath before continuing. 'I don't understand how he got in. My grandmother was downstairs. I screamed and tried to fight him off, but no one came to help me. He hit me over the head with something, and I must've lost consciousness. I thought my grandparents would have come to see me. I don't understand why they haven't. Have you spoken to them?'

'No.' Jemima thought it best to say as little as possible, so as not to have to lie. It was evident that Violet hadn't been informed of her grandmother's murder. 'Do I have your permission to enter your rented house and undertake a search of the property?'

'If you think it would help. Though I don't see what good it will do,' said Violet.

Upon hearing the sound of footsteps, Jemima turned to find a nurse approaching the bed. She had got what she came for, and it was time to leave.

As she strode along the corridor, Jemima saw Broadbent in the distance. He briefly held his hand up to acknowledge her as she closed the gap between them.

'Did you get anything useful from the judge?'

'No, they've sedated him. What about you?'

'Violet's confirmed it was Byron. She's also given us permission to enter and search her property. We'll head there now and start the ball rolling. There's no reason anyone should find out about what we did last night.'

* * *

Minutes after Jemima and Broadbent forced entry into Violet's rented property, she rang Kennedy to tell him about the hidden camera. Jemima asked him to arrange for a technical team to sweep the property to allow all the bugging devices to be located. She also informed him that she and Broadbent intended entering and searching Toombes's house once more. This time, their objective was to search for any evidence that would help them track down Toombes's current whereabouts.

Kennedy told her there was no doubt that Toombes had murdered Cynthia Pickering. His fingerprints were all over the rolling pin used to cave her skull in. There were also bloodied prints on the handrail leading up the stairs, and his bloodstained clothes were discovered in a crumpled heap at the bottom of the Pickering's refuse bin. It was assumed that he had dressed in the judge's clothes before making his escape from the house.

'As Toombes made no attempt to cover his tracks yesterday, it suggests to me that he's confident of evading capture, so he's got to have a plan,' Jemima told Broadbent, once she had finished speaking to Kennedy. 'With that in mind, we're looking for anything which links him to other properties or vehicles. We also want all of his financial records. We know he's intelligent, so it stands to reason that he's considered the possibility that he would eventually get caught out. The sheer volume of recordings suggests he's been at this for quite a while, which means he's had plenty of time to come up with an exit strategy. We just need to find out what it is before he has a chance to go to ground.'

'Easier said than done,' said Broadbent.

'You're not going to get anywhere with that attitude. Everything Toombes does tells us something about him. His actions suggest two things. Firstly, he's extremely confident. Secondly, he has a plan. If Toombes was hanging around the city, then he either has a bolthole nearby, or he's got something here that he needs to retrieve to make his getaway.

'There has to be something here that will give us some insight into his plans. You can start by taking every picture down off the walls. As far as I can recall, they're all framed. We didn't open them up the last time, and there's a chance he could have hidden something inside them. In the meantime, I'm going to head upstairs again.'

A thorough search of the upper floor revealed nothing new. It was disappointing and had clearly been a waste of time. As Jemima finally admitted defeat and headed towards the top of the stairs, she heard Broadbent shout, 'Guv, I've just found a list of passwords! You were right. It was hidden between the frame and the landscape picture hanging in the lounge.'

'Well done, I knew we'd find something,' she said, a sense of relief washing over her.

'Did you find anything upstairs?'

'No, and I think it's about time we headed back.'

Before they left, Jemima turned to scan the property one last time, and something caught her eye. On their previous search of the property, they'd turned up when it was still dark. When the sun had eventually risen, it had been obscured by a blanket of thick cloud. Today the sky was cloudless, and the sun shone through the small glass panel above the front door. The varnish on the treads and risers reflected the natural light, and Jemima noticed an imperfection in the wood.

She walked towards the stairs and bent down to get a better look. There was a slight gap where the base of the third riser should have been flush with the second step. It was no more than a couple of millimetres wide and was uniform across the entire base of the riser. As Jemima used her fingers to feel the join of the wood, she was surprised to find a few small hinges. As she applied pressure towards the middle of the lower section, the riser sprang open.

'Broadbent, look at this!'

'What is it?' He rushed towards where she was crouched.

'It's a hiding place, but I don't know what's in there. Have you got your phone handy? I need some light down here,' she said, pointing excitedly to the open riser.

As the torch illuminated the space, they saw that it contained a box file. Jemima reached in, grabbed the sides and dragged it into the open. 'It's heavy,' she said, as she carried it to the kitchen work surface.

Jemima opened it up. Inside were bundles of fifty-pound notes and numerous documents.

CHAPTER 24

Back at the station, Jemima, Broadbent and Kennedy sat around a large table usually reserved for meetings. The contents of the box file had been tipped into the middle, and Toombes's previously hidden paperwork and cash now lay in a messy heap.

'You don't squirrel away that sort of money if your only source of income is from being a SOCO,' said Broadbent.

'Tell us something we don't know, lad,' said Kennedy. 'Toombes isn't a run-of-the-mill sort of person.'

They each grabbed a handful of paperwork and began studying it. Much of it made no sense, as it appeared to be lists of initials and numbers. As time went by, Jemima's hope of finding something useful was rapidly diminishing — until she picked up a final sheet. Her shriek of triumph caused Kennedy to spill coffee down the front of his shirt.

'He's got a storage unit. It's close to the city centre, near the river Taff,' she said.

'Well, what are you both waiting for? Go!' ordered Kennedy, slamming his hand on the table.

* * *

With Jemima at the wheel, it was a hair-raising journey. She cut the lights and siren before the storage unit came into sight, conscious of the fact that if Toombes was there, it would be counterproductive to announce their arrival.

There were more than a dozen vehicles in the car park, and as they walked into the reception area, Jemima was surprised to find it so busy.

'We can't wait in line,' she said to Broadbent, as she headed to the front of the queue and got out her warrant card. A customer had just taken possession of a key and was walking away, while the next person in line stepped forward to the desk.

'I'm sorry, but you're going to have to wait,' said Jemima. 'This is official police business.'

It took the best part of ten minutes for Jemima and Broadbent to get the information they needed, and for the manager to appear.

'Sorry to have kept you waiting. I'm afraid that I'll have to accompany you. It's company policy,' said the man, as he directed them towards a doorway on the far side of the room.

They soon found themselves in a corridor with a series of doors on each side. Up ahead was a lift. A short distance beyond that was a flight of stairs.

'It's like a maze in here. There're so many different areas. It's the biggest facility of its kind in the city,' gabbled the manager. It seemed he found their presence unnerving. 'The unit in question is three corridors along, but at least it's on this level. So what's your interest in it? Is this man some sort of criminal? Because I can assure you that if he's storing anything illegal in there, we have no knowledge of it. We pride ourselves on being a reputable company.'

Up ahead, the lift pinged as its doors slowly opened and a young couple with a small child emerged. The child raced off along a corridor that Jemima and Broadbent were not yet able to see. 'Harvey, don't go running off!' yelled the boy's father.

'Excuse me! This isn't a playground. You mustn't allow your child to run around like that. It's a health and safety issue!' shouted the manager.

'Get a life, mate,' replied the father of the young boy.

As the five adults came face to face with each other, Jemima could sense that the boy's father was on the verge of losing his temper. She decided to defuse the situation before it escalated. The last thing she needed was to get caught up in a petty dispute when they were racing against the clock.

'Before you say or do anything you might regret, you should know that we're police officers,' she said. She held out her warrant card and saw the man rethink what he was about to do.

'Harvey! Get back here now!' he bellowed, sounding as though he was ordering a dog to heel.

The child skidded to a halt, turned around and raced back towards his parents. As he ran, a side door leading to another corridor opened. A man stepped out without looking. The little boy collided with him, lost his balance and fell to the floor, crying out in surprise.

'I'll have you if you've hurt my son!' shouted the father.

'He shouldn't ha—' began the man, but before he'd finished his sentence, he spun around. The small child had just had enough time to get to his feet when the man started to run, colliding with the child and knocking him to the floor once again.

The mother screamed as her son's head hit the floor. Jemima rushed to the child. She hadn't been able to see the man's face, but she sent Broadbent off in pursuit.

Jemima rushed to check that the child wasn't seriously hurt. It took far longer than she anticipated, as the parents were angry and insistent that she arrest the man responsible for knocking their son out of the way.

Jemima set off along the corridor, running flat out to try to make up for the time she had lost. As she turned the corner, she saw that the corridor turned again about fifty yards further along. Moments later, she heard Broadbent cry out, and realized he must be in trouble.

There was no time to lose.

As she skidded around the next corner, Jemima's blood ran cold. Up ahead was a dead end. More worryingly, Broadbent was on the floor, and the man he'd been chasing was about to bring a wrench down on his head.

'Stop! Police!' she yelled.

Her shout bought Broadbent a few seconds' respite, as the man stopped to glance in her direction. It was Byron Toombes.

'You're not getting out of here, Toombes. I've already called for backup. They'll be here any minute,' she bluffed, continuing to close the distance between them. She could see that Broadbent was in a bad way. He wasn't moving, and blood was pooling around him. 'Give it up, Toombes. You're only making things worse for yourself. You don't want to go down for killing a police officer. I guarantee you'll serve time if you do that. The prison officers will look the other way if the inmates decide to have a go at you. Drop the wrench and give yourself up.'

'The gimp's dead. You're next, bitch!' snarled Toombes.

Jemima swallowed hard. She had no idea whether Toombes was telling her the truth, but whether Broadbent was alive or dead, she had to put him out of her mind.

Toombes raced towards her, brandishing the weapon. The only way she could get out of this situation was to disarm him. Jemima knew that she was fitter and possibly stronger than Toombes, but she was unarmed, and the monkey wrench would do significant damage if he were to get a blow in.

Jemima stood her ground in the centre of the corridor, waiting for Toombes to get close enough to take a swing at her. There was no point trying to talk him down, as the man was intent on inflicting serious damage. The sensible option would have been to turn tail and run. But she needed to come through for Broadbent. She couldn't allow Toombes to make it out of there.

Jemima shifted her weight from foot to foot, like a tennis player standing behind the baseline, waiting until the last moment to anticipate the direction of serve. She kept her eyes on Toombes's face, refusing to blink, hoping it would help her anticipate his intended move.

As Toombes raised his arm, Broadbent's blood trickled down the handle of the wrench. Only a few paces separated them when he brought his arm down in a sweeping arc.

Jemima waited until the last moment to jump out of the way. Her body slammed into the wall, and the wrench missed her.

Toombes was thrown off balance as momentum propelled him on. The weight of the wrench and the movement of his arm caused him to veer off course. As he collided with the wall, he grunted heavily, but somehow he managed to remain upright with his hand still locked around the handle.

Jemima recovered quickly. She was all too aware that this may be the only advantage that she would get. She wasn't as fearful as she might have been, having frequently trained in one-on-one combat situations. Even though Toombes had the weapon, she was confident that he lacked a clear plan. He was forced to improvise to keep hold of his advantage, and Jemima knew just how tiring that could be.

Jemima turned and launched herself at Toombes, intent on disarming him. She was determined not to allow him time to raise the wrench again. She had one arm partially raised as her body connected with his. Her palm forced his jaw upwards as she slammed his head against the wall. There was a sickening thud, which ordinarily should have been enough to stun, but somehow, Toombes managed to lift his arm and drive the wrench into Jemima's ribcage with all the force he could muster.

Agonizing pain shot through Jemima's body, causing stars to appear before her eyes. She opened her mouth to cry out, but the sound died on her lips, as the injury would only allow her to take shallow breaths. Jemima's eyes filled with tears, but she dug deep to rise above the pain. No matter how debilitating it was, she had no intention of giving in to it.

The wrench was a lethal weapon, and Toombes had proved that he wasn't afraid to use excessive force. No matter how difficult it would be, she was determined to hang on to this scumbag. If he broke free now, he'd either kill her or make a run for it. And if he escaped from the corridor, Jemima knew she wouldn't be capable of moving fast enough to apprehend him again.

She had to get the wrench off him, but it was easier said than done. She brought her arm back and punched his face so forcefully that his nose shattered. As one of his hands shot towards his injured face, he momentarily stopped wielding the wrench. His other arm dropped to his side, but his hand remained clamped around the weapon.

Jemima reached out and grabbed the wrench with both hands. It was a high-risk strategy, as only her feet were free.

Quickly changing her centre of gravity, she leaned backwards as she attempted to pull the wrench from his grip. The strategy worked. Toombes's palms were slick with sweat, and the metal slipped from his grasp.

Unfortunately for Jemima, she wasn't quick enough to steady herself. Her feet were too close together, and the floor was far too smooth. The result was inevitable. With nothing to counteract her body weight, she went crashing to the floor. Before she had time to recover, Toombes began to kick her. She did her best to aim some blows at his legs, but as Toombes relentlessly kicked at her ribs, Jemima began to lose consciousness. The pain was worse than anything she'd ever experienced, making it virtually impossible for her to breathe.

A swift kick to the head finished off the attack. As the world slipped away, the last thing Jemima saw was Toombes's boot as it raced towards her face.

PART THREE: 2019

CHAPTER 25

It was clear from their wide-eyed expressions that both Ashton and Peters were shocked to hear what had happened when the team first encountered Byron Toombes.

'I still don't understand how he managed to evade capture. Surely his description had already been circulated?' said Ashton.

'Of course it had, but he'd changed his appearance,' said Broadbent. 'At the time his photograph had been taken, he'd had a thick mop of hair and a beard.'

'Also, we didn't know that he'd been responsible for attacking Huxley and Broadbent,' said Kennedy. 'They were both unconscious when they were taken to the hospital. If either of them had been able to talk, we'd have known immediately that Toombes had changed his appearance. But by the time we were able to view the surveillance footage from the storage unit, he was long gone.'

'What no one realized until a few days later,' Jemima added, 'was that as well as taking some of Douglas Pickering's clothes, Toombes also stole his razor and hair clippers. That's why we didn't immediately realize that we'd found Toombes. He looked completely different. If we'd recognized him, we'd have called it in, and things would possibly have ended differently.'

'The irony of the situation is that if he hadn't panicked when he saw us at the storage unit, he could have kept his head down and walked straight past us. We'd have been none the wiser,' said Broadbent.

'That's right,' Jemima confirmed, 'and what none of us knew is that Toombes had a second vehicle, which enabled him to escape. As you can imagine, Broadbent and I were in a bad way. He was hanging on by a thread. They had him in an induced coma for the best part of a week. I was slipping in and out of consciousness for quite a few hours. It was the following morning by the time I was in a fit state to talk, so Toombes could have quite easily made it out of the country.'

'Locating him was a top priority. But as days turned into weeks, and weeks to months, well . . .' said Kennedy. 'What can I say? We failed. He outsmarted us. If Toombes is behind Violet's disappearance, then we've got our work cut out for us. Just don't make the mistake of underestimating him, because he'll do whatever it takes to get what he wants, and he'll take no prisoners if you stand in his way. In my opinion, he's more dangerous than any other criminal I've come across because he's got inside knowledge. He's spent years working cheek by jowl with us and knows how we think, so if we're going to catch him this time, then we have to be better and smarter. You'll each take a taser. If you get within range, use it. Don't hesitate or warn him. There're to be no half measures.' He turned to Jemima. 'Go and speak to Violet's husband. I'll stay here and coordinate things from this end. Don't forget to keep in regular contact. If you split up after getting the lowdown from Charlie Morgan, I want to know who goes where. No one's to go off the grid.'

* * *

'You drive. I doubt we'll finish on time tonight, so I need to make arrangements for James,' said Jemima, tossing Broadbent the car keys. Ashton and Peters hadn't yet left the building, but as they would be travelling in a separate vehicle they had no need to wait for them.

Broadbent started the engine as Jemima selected her father's number on her phone.

Donald Goodman picked up after three rings, and Jemima could hear the concern in his voice. 'You don't usually ring when you're on shift. Everything all right, Jem?'

'I'm fine, Dad, but something's come up at work and I need a huge favour.'

'You've only to ask. Tell me what you need, and I'll do my best.'

'I know you're already picking James up from school, but I don't know if I'll make it home tonight. We've just taken on a case, and it's time-critical. I was—'

'You don't need to worry, Jem. I'll spend the night at yours if I have to. James and I'll have a boys' night in. I'll order us pizza, and we'll have a game of Risk. He hasn't played that yet, and he's always pestering me about it.'

'Thanks, Dad, that's a weight off my mind. How will you square it with Mum?'

'Don't you worry about her. Celia's my problem. You just get on and do what you have to do, and don't be concerned about James either. I'll make sure he has a great time.'

'I can't guarantee that I'll be back tomorrow night either,' said Jemima. She hated palming James off on others, but her father understood that she was up against it.

'I can pick him up from school tomorrow, but I can't stay with him overnight. Your mother and I have been invited to a little soirée at the Carmichaels. I'm confident about talking her round about my having to stay at yours tonight, but she'd have my guts for garters if I tried to back out of this thing tomorrow. I'm sure Lucy will have him. Leave it with me, Jem. I'll sort it.'

'Thanks, Dad. I'm sorry to drop this on you.' Jemima sighed. She hated putting her father in this position. She knew that despite his making light of things, her mother would give him hell.

'Now go and save whoever it is that needs saving, and I'll speak to you soon.'

When the call ended, Jemima tried to put all thoughts of her mother out of her mind. Celia Goodman was pure poison, though most people didn't see that side of her. She had never accepted James. Even now, with Nick gone, and with Jemima having secured legal custody of James, Celia still refused to see him.

James was too young to know what was going on, but after Nick's dramatic disappearance, Jemima had become more reliant on her family for help. Being a single parent and a police officer often working unpredictable hours was an impossible juggling act. Jemima was grateful her father and sister had been more than happy to step into the breach.

Lucy had been horrified to discover that Celia refused to have anything to do with James, and it had brought her and Jemima closer. It opened her eyes to a side of her mother Lucy hadn't seen before, and made her realize that perhaps Jemima hadn't been exaggerating about their mother treating her less favourably. When Lucy eventually broached the subject with Jemima, it began to heal their long-standing rift.

Jemima snapped her thoughts back to the present as Broadbent pulled up outside Violet's house. Charlie Morgan was standing on the doorstep, eagerly awaiting their arrival. As soon as Ashton and Peters had joined them in the living room, the discussion began in earnest.

'What makes you think that Toombes is behind this?' asked Jemima.

'You worked the case back then. You know all about that creep's obsession with Violet. He stalked then raped her. He killed her grandmother too. The man's a monster, and he's been free to live his life because you let him get away!'

The accusation was out there. Charlie Morgan made no attempt to hide his contempt for the officers who had failed to stop Byron all those years ago. It was nothing that Jemima hadn't thought herself, but hearing someone spit out those damning words with such vehemence still cut her to the quick.

It was particularly hurtful coming from a fellow law enforcement officer, as there would have undoubtedly been occasions throughout Charlie's career when things had not gone to plan and people had suffered because of it. It went with the territory. Even when you did everything possible to get the right result, events happened that were outside your control.

'Violet's the most risk-averse person I know,' Charlie continued. 'There's not a single day that goes by when she doesn't think about that man. She's had to learn to live with the knowledge that he could get to her at any time. I doubt any of you could begin to imagine what it's like to live with that level of fear.'

'You're right,' said Jemima. She lowered her gaze slightly, feeling her cheeks glow with shame.

'Well, lucky you! Ever since I've known her, Violet's been unable to live what the rest of us would call a normal life. She's obsessive about checking in with me, so I can state categorically that she would never do something like this. This isn't a hoax, or Violet trying to make me pay for having to work through the night. Something's happened to prevent her from making contact, and it's not a huge leap to think that Toombes is behind her disappearance.'

'I believe you, and I can assure you that we're proceeding as though that is the case. Has Violet mentioned someone taking an unhealthy interest in her?' asked Jemima.

'No, and as far as I'm aware there hasn't been anyone new in her circle of acquaintants.'

'Was it just Violet and Beth who went out last night?'

'No, it was a group of work colleagues, all women. I don't know their names, but I was going to head over there and see what I could find out.'

'Don't do that. We'll take it from here. I'll need you to stay at home, in case Violet turns up. We'll need the name and address of Violet's place of work, and an address and phone number for Beth's partner. I know you're going to want to do something but leave it to us. Do you have a recent photograph of Violet?'

'Yes, I've already looked one out for you. It was taken about a month ago.'

'That's great. You've done everything you can, so the best thing you can do right now is to try to get some sleep. You look dead on your feet, and you're not going to be of any use later down the line if you're exhausted.'

'But—' began Charlie.

'This isn't a negotiation. Leave it to us, and get some rest,' ordered Jemima. 'I'll be in touch when I know more.'

* * *

Jemima sent Ashton and Peters to Beth's house, while she and Broadbent went to Violet's office. As Broadbent was driving, she used the time to update Kennedy. When the call ended, Jemima realized that Broadbent was unusually quiet. As she glanced across at him, it was apparent that he was lost in thought.

'Toombes?' she asked, already knowing the answer.

'Yeah, I'd hoped we'd seen the last of that bastard. I've never told anyone this, but I still have flashbacks about the attack at the storage unit, especially when I'm stressed. It was the closest I've ever come to losing my life. It was touch and go whether I'd make it and if it wasn't for you . . . Well, I don't need to say it, do I? I owe you my life.'

'If the boot was on the other foot, you'd have done the same for me. Look, I get where you're coming from, but if he's back, we need to deal with him. We're better prepared to face him this time round, so he won't take us by surprise. Plus, as far as I'm concerned, if it is Toombes then there's a hell of a big score to settle.'

'I suppose you're right, but it still scares me. Though, what doesn't make sense is that six years is a hell of a long time to spend waiting to make a move. Surely Toombes isn't still obsessed with Violet?'

'I dunno. The guy's a complete psycho. There's no way to second-guess someone like him.'

'Given Violet's history, I have to agree with Charlie — she wouldn't just disappear without saying something to him. But it seems too far-fetched to think that someone other than Toombes is responsible for her disappearance.'

'I agree, but despite what I said to Charlie Morgan, I think that at this stage we have to keep an open mind. It's not just Violet that's missing. So far, there's no evidence to suggest that it is Toombes. And if we start off focusing entirely on him, and it turns out we've got it wrong, we would have wasted time that could put Violet and Beth in jeopardy.'

When they entered the business premises, Jemima could see that it was a hive of activity. She spoke to the receptionist, explained why they were there, and the woman immediately contacted Denise Pritchard, the head of Human Resources.

Within minutes, Denise arrived. She looked and acted like a corporate dynamo — from her dark suit, short dark hair and designer glasses, to the brisk walk and efficient manner. She quickly dispensed with the pleasantries and ushered them into a waiting room where Jemima explained the seriousness of the situation.

Denise Pritchard was noticeably shocked at the news, and for a moment, her polished professionalism faltered. 'Vi . . . Violet and Beth are well liked members of staff. It goes without saying we'll do anything we can to help. If you follow me, I'll take you to the main office.'

They walked briskly down a narrow corridor lacking any natural light. Denise's stiletto heels sounded like ricocheting bullets as they repeatedly hit the floor. They passed several doors before entering a large, open-plan office where people were busily working away.

'Listen up people, I need your help!' shouted Denise, clapping her hands to ensure that she had everyone's attention. The noise quickly died down, and Denise continued, 'These are police officers. They're here because Violet and Beth went missing last night after spending the evening with some of you. Anyone that was with them last night should go to Meeting Room Three immediately, as these officers are trying to piece together their last known movements. Thank you.'

With that, she turned her attention back to Jemima and Broadbent. 'Follow me. I think it'll be better for everyone concerned if you interview the staff in a separate room. And, if you need any further assistance from me, then I'm only next door.'

The interviews were short and emotional. Everyone was shocked that Violet and Beth had gone missing. Amy confirmed that she'd travelled home on the same bus as them. The missing women had both got off the bus together, while Amy had remained on board. Broadbent made a note of the number of the bus and the approximate timing of events.

Odell informed them that she'd left the pub earlier than most of them as Lisa Randall, who had also been there, had given her a lift home.

When Jemima asked to speak to Lisa, she was informed that the woman had also failed to turn up for work that morning. No one seemed to know where she was.

Jemima thought it was too much of a coincidence that another woman was also unaccounted for. As Broadbent continued to interview the women, Jemima left the room and walked the short distance to Denise Pritchard's office.

When Jemima explained to Denise that Lisa Randall had also been at the pub on the previous night, Denise confirmed that Lisa hadn't come into work that day. More worryingly, she confirmed that she'd not rung in to say that she was sick.

'It says here that her line manager tried to ring her, but she's not answering her phone,' said Denise. 'It's company policy that you ring in by eight o'clock if you're ill. From what I understand, it's quite uncharacteristic behaviour on her part. She's a reliable member of staff. It says in her file that she's married, so you'd have thought that her husband would have rung us if she was too ill to do so herself.'

'I'll need her address,' said Jemima. 'I know she left earlier than the others and gave Odell a lift home, but it's still possible Lisa could be missing too. It's something I'll need to check out.'

Jemima returned to the reception area just as Broadbent stepped out of the interview room. 'I've got Lisa Randall's address,' she said. 'Nobody's seen or heard from her since last night. It's possible we could have three missing women. We should head over there now to find out if that's the case.'

CHAPTER 26

Lisa Randall's house was one of twelve properties set in a small cul-de-sac on the northern edge of Cardiff. As they pulled up outside, Jemima and Broadbent spotted two elderly men perched on stools placed either side of a low wall, separating the drives of their neighbouring properties. One of them looked up and nodded towards the unmarked police car, and the other turned his head to take a look. At another of the properties, an elderly woman was watering a hanging basket. She made no attempt to hide her interest in their arrival.

Jemima and Broadbent got out and checked the house numbers. Lisa lived in number four, which was the second house on the right. They headed up the driveway, Broadbent pressed the doorbell, and they waited.

'You won't get an answer there, mister!' shouted one of the old men. 'She's not in. I know that for a fact, because her car's always on the drive when she's at home.'

'Any idea where she is?' asked Broadbent.

'I haven't got a clue, lad. If I had to take a punt, I'd say she's probably at work.'

'When did you last see her?' asked Jemima.

'Well, before we answer any further questions, I reckon that you two should tell us why you're asking,' said the other elderly man. 'Let's face it, you look respectable enough, but you could be anyone. You hear about fraudsters taking advantage of folks all the time. I'm not that soft. I'm not about to give out details about a young single woman to a couple of strangers.'

'Single?' said Jemima. She turned to Broadbent with a puzzled expression on her face. 'Denise Pritchard told me that Lisa was married.'

The old man stood up suddenly and said, 'If you know what's good for you, I seriously think you two should bugger off before I call the police. I don't know what your game is, but I don't like the way this conversation's going.'

'We *are* police officers,' said Jemima. She showed the men her warrant card. 'I'm Detective Inspector Huxley and that is Detective Sergeant Broadbent. We need to speak with Mrs Randall.'

'She's not married. I've already told you she's single,' said the man, sighing in exasperation. 'She's lived here now for about nine months. And in that time, I haven't seen any man going in or out of that house.'

'And she's not married to a woman either,' added the other man. 'You can ask Brenda over there if you don't believe us,' he said. He pointed at the elderly woman who'd recently been watering her hanging baskets. She'd long since put the watering can down, finding it an unnecessary distraction as she watched what was going on. 'Bren's our very own neighbourhood watch. There's nothing that goes on around here that she doesn't know about. Eh, Bren, get yourself over here and talk to these two police officers.'

Brenda trotted over to join the others.

'Brenda love,' said one of the old men, 'these police officers came to speak with that young woman from number four. They keep insisting she's married.'

'No, she's definitely not married,' replied Brenda, shaking her head emphatically. 'Well, if she is then she's separated from him. I haven't seen any man going in or out of that house since the day she arrived. Mind you, come to think of it, I haven't seen any women go in or out of there either. She's a bit of an oddity — younger than the rest of us and quite the loner. Polite enough, I suppose. Always says hello if she sees me, but she doesn't really talk to any of us. None of us knows much about her, which isn't our way. We don't live in each other's pockets, but we like to feel that we've got a good community spirit here. We look out for one another, but since she's moved in, she keeps herself to herself. But I suppose that's the way with youngsters these days.'

'When did you last see her?' pressed Jemima. It was all very well talking to Lisa Randall's neighbours, but they appeared to have little useful information.

'Ooh, I couldn't say,' said Brenda. 'It's not as though I spend all my time watching the comings and goings around here.'

The two men exchanged glances and chuckled.

'Well, thanks for your time. If by any chance she turns up, then ask her to call me,' said Jemima as she handed the woman her card.

At this stage, they didn't know for sure that Lisa's absence from work that morning was linked to the disappearance of the other two women. Jemima had already established that Lisa had left the pub earlier than all but one other woman, and that woman had arrived home safely. There could be any number of reasons that she wasn't at work or home that morning.

'Well, there's a quarter of an hour of my life I'm never going to get back,' muttered Jemima, as she walked away from the group of pensioners.

'They were harmless enough,' Broadbent chuckled. 'So what do you suggest we do now?'

'Since we're here, we might as well take a quick look around the outside of the property. Take a look through the downstairs windows in case she's holed up inside trying to avoid talking to anyone.'

They had reached the bottom of Lisa's driveway when Jemima's phone rang. 'It's Kennedy,' she said, as she glanced at the screen. 'Go by yourself. I've got to take this.' She spoke into the phone for a few minutes and then hung up, just as Broadbent headed towards her.

'What's up?' he asked.

'Gwent police have found the body of an as-yet-unidentified female. It's in the right age range for it to be either Violet or Beth. I've got to pick up Charlie Morgan to see if he can identify the body. I'll drop you back at the station so that you can get another vehicle to pick up Anton, as he'll need to be there too just in case it's Beth.'

'Can't Fin or Gareth do that?'

'Apparently not. They headed back to the station after they finished speaking to Anton. Kennedy's assigned them to looking over the original case file, in case they find something we overlooked. Can't do any harm, I suppose.

'Did you spot anything out of the ordinary up at Lisa's?'

'Nothing at all. It didn't look as though she was there,' said Broadbent, settling into the passenger seat.

CHAPTER 27

As she pulled up outside Violet's house, Jemima spotted Charlie Morgan at the downstairs window. She was taking the key out of the ignition as he rushed out of the house, eager for news.

'W-what's happened?' he demanded, as he opened the driver's door and bent down to speak to her. The words tumbled out quickly, and the haunted expression on his face betrayed the sense of hopelessness Jemima knew he would be feeling.

She resisted the urge to reach out and squeeze his hand. 'There's no easy way to say this, but I need you to come with me.' Jemima took a deep breath before she continued. 'It could turn out to be unrelated, but Gwent police have informed us that earlier today a woman's body was discovered just off a pull-in on Caerphilly Mountain. She's potentially in the age range to be either Violet or Beth.'

Charlie's breath caught in his throat. He hastily rubbed the back of his hand across his eyes, before forcing himself to stand that little bit more upright. When he next spoke, his voice had lowered, and the words were uttered slowly and deliberately. Jemima appreciated the effort it must take for him not to just fall apart. She thought it admirable and dignified. 'What about Anton?' he asked.

'Sergeant Broadbent has gone to pick him up. I thought it best that you travel separately.'

'Makes sense, I would have made the same call. One of us could end up devastated while the other will be relieved,' said Charlie.

Jemima said nothing. As she drove, she occasionally stole a glance in the rear-view mirror. Charlie sat in silence in the back of the unmarked police car, staring blankly out of the window. After a while he spoke, and Jemima sensed he was desperate not be alone with his thoughts.

'This is all my fault. I let Violet down. I knew what she'd been through and I promised to keep her safe, but last night I put my job first. I was so wrapped up in our latest case that I didn't give her a second thought. What sort of a husband does that make me?'

'You're not to blame, Charlie.'

'Oh yes I am. I should have made arrangements for someone to pick her up, but I didn't. It gave that animal a way to reach her, and now Violet's gone. This is all on me.'

'You weren't to know that anything bad would happen,' said Jemima.

'Well I should have done. I've spent years trying to convince her that Toombes was no longer a threat to her, but now I realize that it was arrogance on my part. I believed that I knew best and kept telling her that she needed to forget about him and move on with her life. I'm such a stupid bastard.

'If I hadn't put my phone on silent, I would have realized sooner that something was wrong. She's my world. I love her to bits. Yet I allowed this to happen. My mistake might have cost Violet her life. At the very least I could have got the ball rolling late last night. I know how important the first few hours are in any missing person case, and I've just fucked up any chance there was of getting her back safely.'

'You don't know that, so stop torturing yourself,' said Jemima. Though she had a feeling that Charlie could be right. Even if the body they were on their way to see turned

146

out not to be Violet's, hours had been wasted and the trail had gone cold. It was almost fifteen hours since anyone had seen or heard from her. You could transport someone a hell of a long way in that time.

Charlie became lost in his thoughts and jumped as Jemima got out of the car and shut the door. Jemima was in no doubt that Charlie's instinct would be to turn away and run as fast as he could, but no matter the outcome, Charlie Morgan had to walk into that building and find out whether Violet was inside. If she was, his world would be blown apart. If she wasn't . . .

Jemima stood aside as Charlie slowly swung his legs out of the car. As he placed his feet on the ground and went to stand, she noticed his legs wobble as though they were about to buckle. She was about to reach out to grab him, but at that moment he closed his eyes, forced his legs to straighten and shut the car door behind him.

Jemima led him to the waiting room, and he followed compliantly. She told him to sit down while she went to the desk and waited as the receptionist placed a call to the relevant department. Jemima glanced at Charlie. He was hunched forward, elbows on knees, head in hands.

Someone eventually came out to inform Jemima that they were moving the corpse to the viewing area.

'What state's the body in?' she asked.

'Not good. There's extensive damage to the head. Is he the person who's come to identify her?' he asked, nodding towards Charlie.

'Yes, and he's only just holding it together.'

'Poor thing. It shouldn't be much longer. They'll be ready for you soon.'

Jemima was reluctant to take a seat near Charlie. It was clear he wanted to be left alone. To help pass the time, she paced slowly back and forth, desperately wishing that she was anywhere other than here. No one liked accompanying relatives to identify a body, but this was by far the worst experience she'd ever had.

Eventually, a sombre-looking grey-haired man headed in their direction. Without introducing himself, he began to speak. 'We're ready for you now, Mr Morgan. I don't know if anyone has explained, but the lady has a head injury, so identification may not be straightforward. Now, if you'd both follow me.'

Charlie didn't acknowledge the man's presence. He remained seated, hunched over and docile.

Jemima walked over to him, crouched down, put a hand on his shoulder and whispered, 'Come on. It's time. I'll be with you every step of the way.'

Charlie looked directly at her as he replied, 'I don't think I can do this. What if it's her? What if it's Violet?'

'You have to do this. You don't have a choice. Come on,' coaxed Jemima, helping Charlie to his feet.

As they walked slowly out of the waiting room, Charlie muttered a desperate prayer, over and over again. 'Please, God, don't let it be Violet. Please, God, don't let it be her.'

When they reached the door of the viewing room, the official turned and spoke once more. 'Would you like to take a moment before you step inside?'

Charlie shook his head. The man opened the door and preceded them into the room. Charlie reached out for Jemima. She put an arm around him, gripping him tightly. When they were all in the confined space, the man closed the door and proceeded to pull back the shroud covering the body.

Charlie took a deep breath and shuffled forward. 'I don't know. I can't tell. Can I take a look at the hands and stomach?' he asked in a trembling voice.

As the official uncovered the cadaver's arms, hands, chest and abdomen, Charlie's knees finally gave way. It took a tremendous effort for Jemima to support his weight and prevent him from falling to the floor. Thankfully, the official wasted no time in grabbing a chair and sliding it beneath him.

Charlie was overcome with emotion. As he sobbed and spluttered, it was just about possible to make out what he was saying. 'I-it's n-not V-Violet. It's not her.'

'Are you quite certain?' asked the man.

'Yes,' nodded Charlie. 'It's not her hands. The wrists are too big, and the fingernails are different. Violet's also got a mole on her stomach.'

Jemima let out a sigh of relief. 'That's good news,' she said, as she squeezed Charlie's shoulder in a show of support.

'Y-you don't understand. I th-think this is Beth.'

Jemima swallowed hard as a lump rose in her throat. This was confirmation that whoever had snatched Violet was prepared to kill. And six years earlier, Byron had demonstrated that he was capable of taking a life by caving someone else's skull in.

CHAPTER 28

As they were approaching the car, Jemima spotted Broadbent's vehicle pulling into the car park. He knew enough not to acknowledge her, as they didn't want to risk Charlie and Anton coming into contact with each other at such a sensitive time. Jemima discreetly gestured that she would call to update him on recent events.

Jemima spotted the glazed expression on Anton's face as the vehicle passed by. She felt wretched knowing what he was about to face.

When they reached the vehicle, Charlie elected to sit in the front passenger seat. It suggested that he might want to discuss the approach they were taking to locate Violet.

Although Jemima was relieved the man's hopes had not been dashed, she needed Charlie to accept that he could have no part in the police operation. 'I'll be with you in a moment,' she said, as she shut the passenger door. She stepped away from the vehicle and selected Broadbent's number on speed dial. Having just cut his engine, she knew he'd be able to answer, and she watched him get out of the car and close the driver's door behind him. He stepped away from the vehicle to ensure that he could not be overheard. It was a surreal situation, speaking to each other on their phones while looking at each other across the car park.

'Charlie's convinced it's Beth,' said Jemima.

'Shit . . . so he's killed again,' said Broadbent.

'If it's him — so far it's just speculation on our part, though it seems the most likely scenario. I'll contact Kennedy and arrange for a FLO to meet you at Anton's. Call me when you've dropped him off. We're against the clock. Let's just hope we're able to figure out where he's gone to ground before he kills Violet.' Jemima disconnected the call and rang Kennedy.

'I'll arrange for a FLO to stay with Charlie too. We don't want him looking over our shoulders, questioning everything we do,' said Kennedy. 'I've got Ashton and Peters looking at Toombes's previous case file — fresh sets of eyes and all that. You never know, they may come up with something.'

'It's definitely worth a try. We should still follow up on Lisa Randall. Before we got pulled away to identify the body, Broadbent and I had called round to her place but there was no one in. I can't put my finger on it, but something feels off. It's too much of a coincidence that she's disappeared off the face of the earth just when Violet and Beth go missing. What if she's been abducted too?'

'I agree. It does seem suspicious. After you've dropped Charlie off, I want you to head back to Lisa Randall's house. If you can't get an answer at the house, I want you to force an entry. For all we know, she could be dead or injured inside that property. I'll get Broadbent to meet you there.'

Before Jemima had a chance to respond, the line went dead.

* * *

The unofficial local neighbourhood watch was curtain-twitching as Jemima pulled into the close. As she got out of the car, she made a point of waving to the elderly woman she had spoken with earlier that day.

Brenda smiled and gestured for her to come over. 'There's been no sign of her. I've been keeping a lookout most of the day. I've kept your card safe so I can call you if I see anything. What are you going to do now? Are you going to break in?' Her eyes were bright with excitement, and the questions tripped off her tongue in her eagerness know what was about to happen.

'I'm afraid I can't discuss an ongoing police operation with you,' said Jemima.

'Understood, officer, understood,' said Brenda, giving Jemima an exaggerated wink. Jemima couldn't help but smile to herself. Brenda would no doubt be glued to the window to ensure that she didn't miss out on anything that happened.

For a frustrating few moments, Jemima repeatedly rang the doorbell and waited. She bent down to peer through the letterbox and noticed a couple of pieces of post. That was more confirmation that Lisa was either not at home, or perhaps incapacitated inside. Though, if it was the latter, she still might have been able to call out and try to attract attention, especially if she heard someone at the door. When it became clear that no one was going to answer, Jemima attempted to look through the windows, but it was impossible to see inside as blinds obscured the view. She stood still and listened intently. There appeared to be no one at home.

Jemima knew that she should wait for Broadbent to arrive, especially if Byron Toombes was holed up inside the property, but she had a taser and was more than prepared to use it. The desire to get on and do something had mounted to such a level that Jemima was prepared to risk forcing an entry while she was on her own. She headed towards the side of the property, walked further up the drive, and opened the side gate. A quick look through the rear windows told her that no one was home. The back door had a clear glass pane and Jemima spotted a key in the lock.

Jemima found a large stone to smash the pane of glass. She knocked out the sharp edges and reached in to open the door. As she scanned the galley kitchen, she was struck by how neat it was. With nothing out of place, it almost looked staged. A door at the far end led to a small hallway, where a few envelopes lay on the floor. To her right was another door, which led to the main living area. As she stepped inside, she noticed that the showroom effect had continued in this room, with the trappings of a very comfortable existence. There was a Bose music system, a large flat-screen TV and modern prints on the walls, but the place lacked a lived-in feel, as there were no personal effects.

When she heard a noise coming from the direction of the kitchen, Jemima felt her body tense. Her fingers moved towards the taser. 'Police! Who's there?' she shouted.

'Only me,' said Broadbent.

'I thought you'd never get here.' Jemima breathed a sigh of relief. She quickly put her hand down to a natural resting position.

'Impatient as ever — you could've waited.' Broadbent strode into the room.

'Not really. Now you're here, you can help me search this place. I haven't had a chance yet, but I've a feeling Lisa's not here. We need to find a photograph of her to take back to the station. There're no personal effects down here. It's too bloody neat and tidy. I mean, who the hell lives like this?'

'Let's make a start upstairs,' suggested Broadbent. 'We don't want to hang about for too long.'

As they headed upstairs, a bathroom was immediately in front of them. Just like the other rooms, it was neat. The only items on display were a glass containing a solitary toothbrush and a neatly squeezed tube of toothpaste standing on the window ledge. There was also a disposable razor and a can of shaving foam.

There were three bedrooms, the smallest of which had been set up as a study. It contained two filing cabinets, a corner desk that housed a computer, and a large, comfortable-looking, leather-effect swivel chair. Jemima tried to open the filing cabinets, but they were both locked.

The second bedroom was completely empty and was neither curtained nor carpeted. The main bedroom was by far the largest of the rooms. There was a king-sized bed, covered in luxurious-looking bedding. The pillows were plumped, and the duvet looked pristine.

'No way!' cried Broadbent, as he walked over to a large pine chest of drawers.

'What's the matter?' asked Jemima. She followed him and immediately noticed an ornately framed wedding photograph of Lisa and her husband.

'It's him! It's Toombes,' Broadbent said. 'This isn't a coincidence. He must have snatched Violet and murdered Beth.'

'I'll ring Kennedy,' said Jemima. Her heart rate had increased, and she was unable to stop shaking as she spoke down the phone: 'We need every available officer on this. Lisa Randall's married to Toombes. We need a team down here now to take this house apart.'

CHAPTER 29

Kennedy wasted no time in arranging for a team of officers to head to Lisa Randall's house. This was proof that Toombes had played a part in both Violet's disappearance and Beth's murder, and it significantly lowered the odds of them finding Violet unharmed.

It puzzled Jemima that Byron had gone on to have a long-term relationship. Experience had shown Toombes to be a violent obsessive. It made Jemima wonder whether or not Lisa was a victim of coercive control, and as Byron continued to be obsessed with Violet, there was a real possibility that Lisa could find herself surplus to requirement.

'Do you see what I see?' asked Jemima, as she stared at the framed wedding photograph.

'Yeah, it's freaky, but she looks a hell of a lot like Violet. I wonder if she always looked like that, or did he make her change her appearance?' said Broadbent.

'My thoughts exactly . . .'

If Lisa had only just discovered that she was Byron's consolation prize, it was impossible to second-guess the effect it would have on her. If she loved her husband, she could feel compelled to hurt or even kill Violet, as she would see her colleague as a rival for his affection.

Without any obvious way of knowing the actual state of their marriage, Jemima endeavoured to use everything she knew about Toombes to allow her to make an educated guess. The illegal surveillance tapes discovered during their previous encounter with him showed that he had gone to great lengths to indulge his proclivity for voyeurism. The sheer volume of recordings demonstrated that it was more than just a passing phase. Toombes was a hardened voyeur, which suggested that he would have difficulty maintaining a healthy sexual relationship with a long-term partner. For him to tie himself to Lisa didn't make sense.

It seemed highly unlikely that Lisa was a willing accomplice in these recent events. Prior knowledge of her husband's obsession with Violet could have had a devastating effect on Lisa. It would have required an exceptional level of self-control for her to regularly interact with her rival in a work-based situation without raising suspicion, and as far as Jemima knew, there had been no suggestion that anyone had sensed animosity between the two women. This implied that until the abduction, Lisa had been unaware of any link between Byron and Violet.

Jemima turned to Broadbent. 'I'm going to try to jimmy the lock on the filing cabinet. I haven't been able to find the key, and we need to see what's inside. Give me a hand. It'll be quicker with two of us.'

Forcing the cabinet proved to be far from easy, but after numerous attempts and a lot of brute force, they eventually managed to prise it open. Inside were a couple of laptops, a handful of memory sticks and more surveillance equipment. It was definitive proof that Byron was up to his old tricks. There was also a drawer containing DVDs labelled with the initials VW.

'I see that being in a long-term relationship doesn't appear to have tempered his appetite,' said Broadbent.

'They must be recordings of Violet. We didn't find any of them back then because he'd hidden them in a safe place,' said Jemima.

'Either that, or he's filmed her more recently,' said Broadbent, shaking his head in despair. 'Lisa must've known what he was up to. Let's face it, sticking these in a locked cabinet is hardly an attempt at hiding things. Though, she could be into voyeurism too. She could have taken that job to enable them to get close to Violet. Otherwise, it's too much of a coincidence.'

'We need to get everything looked at now. As soon as the search team arrives, I'll send an officer back to the station with this lot. I'll call Ashton and tell him to drop whatever he's up to. We know Toombes has exceptional technological skills. He's probably encrypted any incriminating files. With Ashton's degree in Computer Forensics, he's best placed to find out what secrets Toombes has been hiding. If we're lucky, something here might give us the location of where he's taken Violet.'

When the team of officers arrived, Jemima allocated tasks to ensure that they carried out a methodical search of each room. The contents of the filing cabinet were recorded, placed in evidence bags and transported to the station.

It took a couple of hours to complete a thorough search of the house. When Jemima and Broadbent eventually arrived back at the station, they found a few officers huddled around a TV. Although familiar, they were not regular squad members.

'What are you doing?' asked Jemima.

'The DCI said you needed help, so we've been shunted across to do what's necessary. We've started with this. That Toombes is deffo a perv, guv,' said one of the officers, making no attempt to hide a salacious smile. 'We've found loads of hardcore porn films, just like this one,' he said, pointing at the screen. 'I can't believe some of the things he was into. You wouldn't think half of it was physically possible. It's been a proper—'

'I'm only going to say this once,' snapped Jemima. 'This is neither the time nor place for puerile behaviour. It doesn't take four of you to watch those films. One woman's been murdered, and at least one other's missing. So do your jobs or piss off home and wait for your P45s to arrive in the post. Do we have statements from residents living in the vicinity of the stop where the women got off the bus?'

'Not yet. I was just about to make a start on it,' muttered PC Quentin, staring at the floor as he spoke. His cheeks reddened with embarrassment under Jemima's steely glare.

'Don't you realize that we're running out of time?' she shouted.

'No, ma'am. I mean, yes, ma'am,' he replied, shifting his weight from foot to foot as though he was standing on hot coals.

'Get out of here and do your job! And that goes for the rest of you!'

'Oh, I nearly forgot,' said PC Porter, 'DCI Kennedy called earlier to say that there's a press conference organized for five o'clock. He expects you to be there. They've agreed to cover the case on the local news this evening.'

'Why didn't you tell me about that straight away?' said Jemima as she glanced at her watch. 'That only leaves me thirty minutes.' She turned around. 'And what are you *still* doing here, Quentin? Get those interviews done. A woman's life could depend on it.'

Jemima headed for her locker and freshened herself up before heading downstairs for the press conference. With the size of the crowd attending the previous night's football game, she hoped that it would jog some memories. Hopefully someone would have noticed the two women getting off the bus and could give the detectives the lead they so desperately needed.

CHAPTER 30

The press liaison officer had already prepared a carefully worded statement about how and when the two women were abducted.

Jemima then explained how Violet had previously been stalked by Toombes. 'I want to emphasize that at this stage of the investigation we cannot categorically say that Byron Toombes is behind the disappearance of these women. However, evidence gathered so far would suggest that it is a strong possibility.'

A collective whisper rose as reporters sensed that this could be a bigger story than they had originally anticipated. An image of Byron appeared on a screen and there was a flurry of activity. Hands were raised and people began to shout out questions.

'There'll be plenty of time for questions later.' The press officer cleared her throat and made herself heard above the crowd. 'Settle down. Please allow the inspector to continue.'

Jemima cleared her throat before speaking. She was fully aware that this was the ideal opportunity to get the message out there and alert the public to what had happened. It was a high-stakes roll of the dice that could result in the break-through they were so desperate for. The flip side was that it would inevitably bring the time-wasters and attention-seekers out of the woodwork.

'This is the latest image we have of Byron Toombes.' Jemima pointed to the screen. 'As it was taken six years ago it's likely that he may have changed his appearance. I would emphasize that this man is known to be dangerous. Anyone who sees him should not approach him but contact the station immediately on this dedicated line.' A telephone number appeared on the screen.

Reporters began shouting out questions. Jemima fielded them as best she could, and things went reasonably well until one member of the press asked for confirmation of whether the body of a female recently found murdered on Caerphilly Mountain was either Violet Watkins or Beth Stanton. At that point, the press liaison officer ended the press conference.

Jemima walked briskly from the room, ignoring the sound of journalists shouting questions in the hope that she would turn around and answer them. She was glad it was done with, and headed to the operations room where Ashton was hard at work.

'How's it going?' she asked.

'Nothing so far. Toombes is careful and certainly knows his stuff. There's highly sophisticated encryption in place. It'll take time, but I'm sure I'll get there.'

'Well, time's something we don't have. I know you're doing everything you can, and there's no one better placed than you to get into that machine, but please work faster, Finlay. That bastard caved Beth Stanton's skull in. He's got to be holding Violet somewhere. If we don't find her soon, she's probably going to end up on a slab too.'

A break came almost an hour later when someone discovered a list of telephone numbers in a battered old notebook. There had been a very basic telephone in Lisa Randall's house, which didn't have a last number redial facility on it. They'd contacted British Telecom to ask for a record of any calls made from the line but had been informed that they only provided the line rental. A search of available paperwork showed that bills were likely to have been paid online. Gareth Peters had been assigned the task of establishing which telecoms company the contract was with.

'Guv, I think I've found a telephone number for either Lisa's or Byron's mother,' said DC Davies, rushing over to Jemima's desk.

'Good work, Davies. This could be just the break we need. It is likely to be Lisa's mother. I seem to recall that Byron's parents had already died when he first came to our attention.' Jemima reached for the notebook, dialled the number and let it ring out. She was just about to hang up when the call was answered.

'Hello,' said a frail-sounding voice.

'Hello, I'm Detective Inspector Jemima Huxley from South Wales Police. I'd like to . . .'

'Has something happened to my Lisa?' asked the woman. 'Are you her mother?'

'Of course I am. What's happened to her? What's wrong?'

'Your daughter's missing. No one seems to know where she is. And we must speak to her as soon as possible. We can't locate her husband either. Have you heard from either of them lately? Or do you have any idea where they're likely to be?'

'Her husband died about a year ago, Inspector. It happened on one of their visits back to this country. He got run over by a lorry in London. My Lisa's never been the same since then. It changed her. I could never understand why she married him. You see, I never liked him, and Lisa knew it. I don't know what it was, but he was a wrong 'un. He'd flash the cash, act all pleasant like, but there was something not right behind those eyes of his. But Lisa wouldn't have a word said against him. If you listened to her, you'd think he was a saint.

'She was inconsolable for months after he died, and then out of the blue, she turned herself around. She moved back to Cardiff and set her mind on getting a job at that office of hers. It took a while, but she held out until she got offered one. As far as I know, she's doing quite well for herself. Not that she needs the cash. If she never worked at all, she'd still have more money than most people.'

'When was the last time that you spoke to Lisa, Mrs Randall?' interrupted Jemima in an attempt to regain control of the conversation. The woman spoke so rapidly that she barely had time to draw breath.

'Why are you calling me Mrs Randall? My Lisa is Mrs Randall. I'm Mrs Pettigrew, and my Lisa was a Pettigrew before she got married.'

Jemima puzzled over what the woman had just said. If Lisa was married to Byron, she would have either kept her original surname or have taken the name Toombes. Before she had time to say anything, the woman continued with her narrative.

'Let me see . . . It must have been about a week ago. Lisa didn't say that she was going anywhere. But perhaps she's gone off with one of her friends at that office where she works. She's been a lot happier since she's been there. She even said that she's starting to get over David's death.'

'Who's David?' asked Jemima.

'Her husband, of course. You don't think anything awful has happened to her, do you?'

'So your daughter Lisa was married to a man named David Randall?'

'That's right.'

'Was she ever in a relationship with someone named Byron Toombes?'

'No.'

'Are you certain?' asked Jemima.

'I know I'm old, but I'm not completely gaga.'

'I'd like to call round and show you a photograph of Lisa. So could I have your address?'

'I'm not giving you my address. After all, you could be anyone. You could just be pretending to be a police officer.' And with that, the woman ended the call.

Jemima looked up to find every eye in the room upon her.

'What's up?' asked Broadbent.

'Apparently Lisa Randall was married to David Randall, who supposedly died last year. Lisa's mother — Mrs Pettigrew — has never heard of anyone named Byron Toombes.'

'So what're we going to do?' asked Broadbent.

'We need to show Lisa's mother the photograph of her daughter and Toombes. But first of all, we need to find out where Mrs Pettigrew lives. The woman wouldn't give me her address because she thought I was some kind of con artist.'

'I'll look into that,' said Peters. 'Pettigrew isn't a common name in this part of the country, so I should be able to track her down.'

'But what good is it going to do showing her that photograph?' asked Broadbent.

'I've no idea. But Lisa has a connection with Toombes, whether her mother knows it or not. I suppose it's possible she married him after her first husband died, and perhaps her mother doesn't know about it. Right now, we don't have anything else to go on, so it's worth following it up.'

Twenty minutes later, they had an address for Mrs Pettigrew.

CHAPTER 31

Jemima and Broadbent pulled up outside Mrs Pettigrew's house and she opened the door.

'Mrs Pettigrew, I'm Detective Inspector Huxley from the South Wales Police, and this is Detective Sergeant Broadbent. We spoke earlier on the telephone about your daughter, Lisa.'

'Yes, I remember,' she said, after she examined their warrant cards. 'I'm sorry I hung up on you. I was just a bit scared. You hear such awful things, and I let my imagination run away with me. Anyway, I know who you are now, so come on in. I'm very concerned about Lisa going missing like this. It came as a bit of a shock when you called me earlier. I'll do anything I can to help. I just want my Lisa to be found. She's the only family I've got left now. Her father died when she was seven, and I never remarried. I'm a one-man woman you see — always have been, and always will be. My poor Alex would be turning in his grave now if he knew that our precious little girl was missing.'

'Mrs Pettigrew, I've brought along a photograph of your daughter that I'd like you to take a look at. I need to know if you recognize the man she's with,' said Jemima. She held out the framed wedding photograph they'd taken from Lisa's house.

Mrs Pettigrew reached for the photograph. 'Yes, I know him. It's Lisa's husband, David. Why are you so interested in him? I've already told you that he's dead.'

'You're saying that this man is David Randall?' asked Jemima.

'Yes, who else could it be?' The woman looked at Jemima as though she'd said something ridiculous.

'We know him as Byron Toombes,' said Broadbent.

'Are you sure he's dead?' pressed Jemima.

'As sure as I can be. I didn't see his body, but Lisa was devastated. Is this your way of telling me that David was up to no good and that he's very much alive and has put my Lisa in danger?'

'After what you've just told us, I don't know what to think,' said Jemima. 'The only thing I'm able to say is that your son-in-law is known to us, and we need to speak to him in connection with an ongoing investigation.'

'Oh my word!' squealed Mrs Pettigrew. 'Are you saying he's not dead? Is my Lisa in danger?'

'Truthfully, I've no idea.'

'What's he done?'

Jemima could see the panic in the woman's eyes. 'I'm afraid that we're unable to discuss an ongoing investigation, Mrs Pettigrew.' She knew it was an unsatisfactory answer but was not prepared to divulge information and risk compromising the case.

'You have to promise me that you'll find my Lisa.'

'That's our intention, and it's why we're here. But we need your help.'

'Just tell me what you need. I'll do anything.'

'Do you have any photographs, letters or postcards that Lisa may have sent you since she got married?' Jemima asked. 'Anything which could potentially give us a clue as to her current whereabouts? We think she might have gone somewhere outside of the city. Possibly somewhere remote.'

'Oh, I can't think,' said Mrs Pettigrew. 'My mind's gone blank. Wait a minute . . . Yes, she's got a holiday cottage!'

Jemima's heartrate increased, though she kept her voice level. 'Where exactly is this cottage?'

'I can't remember where it is.' The elderly woman sounded pained as she uttered the words.

'We really need to know, Mrs Pettigrew. I can't over-emphasise how important this could be. It's crucial that we locate Lisa.'

'I know. I know. I'm doing my best. Just give me a moment . . . I've lots of keepsakes in a box at the bottom of my Welsh dresser. Perhaps that would help?'

'Yes, if we could just take a look, we might find something that would help us find the place,' said Jemima.

* * *

Mrs Pettigrew showed them into a small, cluttered room, where ornaments appeared to fill every bit of available space. The room was far too hot, and the air stale, as if the windows were rarely opened. There were an oversized sofa and armchair, which looked as though they had seen better days. A large coffee table dominated the central area. The carpet was threadbare in places, and the floral wallpaper faded and peeling.

The old woman hobbled slowly as she negotiated her way around the furniture. As she reached the dresser, she opened one of its drawers and pulled out a box stuffed full of papers.

'I expect you'll want to make a start looking through these? I'm going to make a cup of tea. You're in luck because I bought a packet of chocolate digestives this morning. I always think it's nice to have a treat now and again.' The woman seemed pleased to have company and kept talking even after she'd walked out of the room. Busying herself with a mundane activity was undoubtedly a coping strategy to take her mind off the fact that her daughter was missing, and quite possibly in danger.

'Come on, we haven't got time to waste,' said Jemima, grabbing a handful of papers from the box.

'Have a heart — she's old, lonely and confused,' said Broadbent in a hushed tone. 'Just don't try to rush her, or she might clam up altogether. If she happens to recall anything useful, it's more likely to come out with a bit of cajoling rather than by taking a more direct approach. Perhaps you should let me do the talking while you look through that stuff? I think we're likely to get more out of her that way.'

'Fine by me,' muttered Jemima.

'I'll give you a hand, Mrs Pettigrew,' called Broadbent, as he headed towards the kitchen.

'There's really no need, young man.'

'Nonsense,' he replied. 'I'd like to help. I also thought that we could have a bit of a chat while you're pouring the tea. Inspector Huxley's getting on fine without me.'

'Well, I have to say it will be nice to have someone to talk to. I seem to spend so much time by myself these days. A lot of elderly neighbours have passed away now. The young-sters that have moved in, well . . . they're not the same. Half of them won't give you the time of day. They're too full of their own self-importance.'

From where she sat on the sofa, Jemima could clearly hear the conversation. She was glad that Broadbent had sug-gested that he should go and speak to her. It allowed Jemima time to search through Mrs Pettigrew's paperwork, and she was able to listen in on Broadbent's fact-finding mission.

'Does Lisa come to visit you often?' asked Broadbent.

'She doesn't,' sighed Mrs Pettigrew. 'We were close until that husband of hers came along. Of course, before he came on the scene she lived across the other side of the world, but she was always on the phone to me. He changed her. I knew from the moment I met him that no good would come from that relationship. I told her that he wasn't the right man for her. There was something about him that I just couldn't take to. I couldn't put my finger on it straight away, but I sensed there was something not quite right about him.

'They were always flitting here, there and everywhere. It wasn't right. I went to stay with them once, at one of their houses in London. He had a padlock on one of their bedroom doors. I asked my Lisa about it. She said it was his office, and he didn't want anyone disturbing things in there. She'd never been allowed in there herself. There shouldn't be secrets between husband and wife.'

'How did Lisa seem after her husband's death?' asked Broadbent.

'Oh, she was pitiful. Lisa was in no fit state to do anything. I moved in with her for a few months. She had no interest in anything. The doctor wanted to give her some tablets to help her sleep, but she wouldn't take them. I was worried about her. She'd lie on the bed crying her heart out. "Who's Violet?" she kept asking, over and over again. It didn't make any sense. I told her that I didn't know anyone called Violet.

'One afternoon, I heard this awful noise on the landing. It was Lisa. She was breaking into that locked room of his. How she managed to stay sane after that, I'll never know. He had the most awful things in there. There were homemade films of a woman getting undressed, taking a shower, and doing disgusting things on a bed. Well, it was easy to see what sort of woman she was. No decent person would ever let themselves be filmed like that. That woman had no sense of shame.

'Then we found some women's underwear, and it wasn't my Lisa's. They weren't even big enough to cover her sense of shame. They must have belonged to that floozy.

'As you can imagine, it was enough to send my Lisa over the edge. She'd just lost a man that she was totally devoted to, only to find out in such a cruel way that he'd been carrying on a sexual relationship with a common slut.

'I was at my wit's end, seeing my little girl in pain like that. I didn't know what to do for the best. The only thing I knew for sure was that Lisa couldn't carry on the way things were. After a lot of soul-searching, I suggested that she should try to find this woman, and tell her exactly what she thought of her. I was sure that once she'd got all the upset out of her system, she could start to put everything behind her.'

'Violet didn't do anything to hurt your daughter, Mrs Pettigrew. She's an ordinary young woman, who unfortunately became your son-in-law's next-door neighbour,' said Broadbent.

Jemima headed into the kitchen. 'We've seen the recordings, Mrs Pettigrew. They were taken six years ago, when your son-in-law was terrorizing Violet Watkins. We worked the case at the time. You say Byron's—'

'My son-in-law was David, not—'

'You say he's dead, but you didn't see his body,' continued Jemima. 'At the moment we've no proof that your son-in-law is dead, but we know that he's a dangerous man. We also know that your daughter is missing. What we're unclear about is whether Lisa is being held against her will.'

'Oh, dear God, no!' shrieked Mrs Pettigrew. The colour drained from her cheeks as she clamped her hands over her mouth. Broadbent placed a supportive arm around her, and the woman leaned into him.

'I need you to focus, Mrs Pettigrew,' continued Jemima. 'Do you know of anywhere that your daughter could be?'

'She could be anywhere. David had hundreds of properties all over the world.'

Jemima's mouth hung open in disbelief. Six years ago, they had been unable to trace who was behind the series of shell companies who owned both Violet's and Byron's properties and numerous others. Now it seemed a certainty that they were actually Byron's. It explained how he had been able to access so many different properties to unlawfully record the most personal moments of young women's lives.

'Was there any particular property that they spent time at as a couple? The cottage you mentioned, is it somewhere close to here, but perhaps a bit secluded?'

'Oh, I don't know,' cried Mrs Pettigrew. 'This has all come as such a shock. I'm just so flustered.'

'Think, Mrs Pettigrew,' encouraged Jemima. 'Anything that you could tell us, no matter how small or insignificant it seems, could potentially help us find them.'

'No, no, there's nothing,' she replied, shaking her head. 'Oh, wait a minute, Lisa did say that you could see the highest point in South Wales from the back of the house, but I don't know where that is.'

'I've just flicked through some of your photographs. One of them had mountains in the background. I thought it might have been taken somewhere in the Brecon Beacons. I'm sure I recognized Pen y Fan,' said Jemima.

'Yes, that's it! Rose Cottage — that's where they used to go. They took me there once, and I spent the weekend with them. I forgot about that photograph. I seem to forget a lot of things these days.'

'Do you have an address or a telephone number so that we can try to locate the cottage?'

'No. When Lisa stays there, she always rings me from one of the payphones in the local pub. She doesn't even have a mobile phone. I know it's somewhere out in the country. It's easy to get lost out there as there're hardly any houses and lots of lanes that seem to go nowhere.'

CHAPTER 32

As they raced towards the car, Jemima tossed the keys to Broadbent. 'You drive. I've got a lot to organize,' she ordered.

'Back to the station?' he asked.

'No, head for the A470. We're going towards Brecon.'

'But we don't know for certain that Violet's there.' Broadbent sighed heavily. It seemed Jemima was intent on taking them both on a wild goose chase.

'She must be there, Dan. Think about it. We know that Beth was found on Caerphilly Mountain. That's north of the city. Keep going and you eventually get to Brecon.'

'You're clutching at straws. You can get to any number of places from there.'

'I'm asking you to trust me on this. It's not a huge leap to think that if Toombes has got Violet, he'll take her somewhere remote. And that cottage would fit the bill. We're running with this because I'm the senior officer and I believe I'm right.' Jemima immediately felt churlish for pulling rank. She could understand Broadbent's scepticism. Yet despite not having any solid evidence to back up her hunch she was convinced that she was right.

'If it ends up that I've called it wrong then I'll hold my hands up and there'll be no blowback on you. I'll let

Kennedy know about Rose Cottage. He can contact Dyfed-Powys Police and tell them to expect us.' Jemima dropped on to the front passenger seat and slammed the door shut.

'It'll take us well over an hour to get there, and we don't have the location of that cottage,' protested Broadbent.

'That's why we need to get going. We can't afford to waste time. Dyfed-Powys has a far better chance of locating the place. They can also organize an Armed Response Unit. If they get moving straight away, everything should be in place by the time we arrive.'

Once they'd made it off the local roads, they headed north along the A470, sticking to the fast lane. Blue lights flashing, siren blaring. It was late enough to have missed the rush hour logjam, but the road was still incredibly busy. Thankfully there had been no accidents earlier in the day, and drivers up ahead switched lanes to allow them to pass.

Jemima put the call on speakerphone as she spoke to Kennedy. She made no attempt to disguise the frustration in her voice, which was in marked contrast to Kennedy's calm, matter-of-fact tone. Being a police officer was more than just a job to Jemima. She did her utmost to ensure that every victim got justice, and sometimes felt as though she was an avenging angel. After Jemima disconnected the call, they sat in silence, until Kennedy rang back to update them on progress at his end. Dyfed-Powys Police had been made aware of the situation and were expecting them, but no one seemed to know the whereabouts of Rose Cottage. Kennedy assured them that Dyfed-Powys Police were optimistic that they would be able to locate the cottage. The only problem was that they were running out of time.

Jemima tapped her leg distractedly as she stared out of the window. 'Can't you drive any faster?' she asked.

'I'm going as fast as I can. This road isn't the easiest and I don't know about you, but I don't have a death wish,' said Broadbent.

'Neither do I, but we may not get there in time,' she snapped.

'Firstly, no one knows where the cottage is. Secondly, if I go any faster, we might not get there at all, so stop having a go, and let me concentrate on the driving,' said Broadbent.

'I'm just struggling to remain detached. We know Violet, and we owe her because we let her and her grandparents down. Toombes should have spent the last six years rotting away in a prison cell but instead, he's been living the dream. It makes me sick. We're to blame for all of this. We should have sorted it back then. And I'm damned if I'm going to let Byron bloody Toombes get one over on us again.'

'We did everything we could possibly do back then,' said Broadbent. 'Don't forget, it ended badly for both of us. If it hadn't have been for you, I'd most likely have ended up six feet under. And after I lost consciousness, you took a hell of a beating. No one could have done more. You held that bastard off, and I owe you my life.

'I don't think I've ever told you this, but up until that afternoon I still resented you. I'd tried to get over it, but every so often it would spill out, and I'd let it get the better of me. I hated the fact that you'd made sergeant and I was still a DC. I really believed they'd made a mistake, that they'd been easy on you because you're a woman and they needed to meet their quota. A lot of the guys were dripping poison in my ear. And it was easier to believe that that's why you got the promotion instead of me. Thinking that was better than facing up to my own inadequacies. In hindsight, I feel ashamed of how I treated you back then.'

'Yeah, you were a right dick,' said Jemima.

'Oh cheers,' said Broadbent, as his cheeks flushed with embarrassment.

'Forget about it, Dan. You're talking about things that happened so long ago that they no longer matter.'

'It may not matter to you, but it matters to me. I feel ashamed of myself when I think back on how I gave you such a hard time. The truth is, you deserved to be a sergeant, and I didn't. It kills me to say it, but you're twice the officer I'll ever be. I know I'm not the brightest, but I am loyal, and as far as I'm concerned you're the best.'

'Enough of the gushing sentimentality,' said Jemima with a coy smile. It felt good to know that Broadbent looked up to her.

'Fair enough, but I just want you to know that I'll always have your back.'

'That's good to know. But let's hope it never comes to that. One of the reasons I'm so involved in this case is because I've had a strange feeling recently that someone is watching me. I don't know whether it's because I half expect Nick to show up, or whether I'm just being paranoid,' said Jemima.

'Nick won't come back. He's not stupid. He'll know there's a warrant out for his arrest after skipping his trial. So you don't need to worry on that score,' said Broadbent.

'I s'pose.' At the mention of her husband's name, Jemima's thoughts were momentarily cast back to the time when their marriage imploded. During those last few weeks together, the man she had fallen in love with all but disappeared. It seemed that almost overnight Nick had become an ugly drunk who would take out his unhappiness on Jemima and James. He had behaved appallingly, and she knew that she could never forgive him.

'Has any specific incident made you feel that you're being watched?'

'Nothing I can put my finger on. It's just a feeling. I'm probably blowing things out of all proportion. In fact, I definitely am. Violet is the one who's been stalked, and I'm projecting her circumstances on to me.'

'Don't dismiss things so quickly,' said Broadbent. 'When you think of all the people we've put away over the years, we're bound to have plenty of enemies. If I were you, I'd trust your intuition, and perhaps be a bit more vigilant. If anything seems suspicious, day or night, then you call me. Like I said, I'll always have your back.'

'Caroline will love that,' said Jemima, referring to Broadbent's wife.

'Believe me, Caroline knows the score. There won't be any complaints from her,' said Broadbent.

Away from signs of human habitation, the darkness enveloped them at an alarming speed. Apart from their headlights, there was no sign of light, and the long and winding road seemed to go on for ever.

'We're almost at the Dyfed-Powys headquarters,' said Jemima.

Broadbent let out a sigh of relief.

Jemima was out of the car before he had time to switch off the engine, and she raced into the reception area.

It took a while for anyone to come to see them. As the minutes ticked away, Jemima became increasingly agitated. Eventually someone appeared, and they were taken through to the operations room, where they were introduced to Detective Inspector Dawn Rudd, who was the officer in charge.

'Have you located the cottage yet?' asked Jemima.

'We've contacted the Royal Mail and the Land Registry. Unfortunately, this is outside the operating hours of the Land Registry, but we eventually managed to get hold of someone. When we explained the seriousness of the situation, they said that they'd arrange for the appropriate person to go in and search the database. The Royal Mail has come up with a couple of possibilities which we're in the process of checking out.'

'This is taking far too long. Don't you understand that Violet Watkins could die? There's got to be a quicker way,' said Jemima.

'If you've got any better suggestions, then I'm happy to hear them,' replied Dawn Rudd, though her voice and body language suggested otherwise. 'I can assure you we're doing everything we can with the resources that are available to us.'

'I'm sure you are, but—' interrupted Jemima.

'But nothing. This isn't the city. We've a large area to cover, and don't have much to go on. It would have been far easier if you could have narrowed down the search area, but as you haven't even given us the name of a village, we have to consider every possibility and discount things as we go along. What I can tell you is that we will locate the property. It's just a matter of time.'

'But it's time we don't have. Violet Watkins's life is in danger. Her companion has already been murdered and dumped on a hillside. But Violet was always the primary target.'

'Don't give me a hard time. We're on the same side here, and I understand your concerns. Everyone's working as quickly as they can. I've got our best team on this. We all want to find the victim and get her out of there safely.'

Jemima didn't bother to reply. She knew that it was unreasonable to be so impatient but no matter how hard she tried, she couldn't stop thinking that they'd be too late to save Violet. And if that turned out to be the case, Jemima didn't believe that she would be able to forgive herself. Their failure to get Byron Toombes sent down the first time had ultimately set off this chain of events. If Toombes had been sent to prison six years earlier, he would not have met Lisa Randall. Violet would not have been stalked again, and Beth would still be alive.

There was no option but to wait and hope that someone located Rose Cottage in time for them to save Violet. Jemima did the only thing she could think of, and paced the room like a caged bear, periodically glancing at the clock on the wall.

'We've got a result, people!' shouted someone from the far side of the room. 'The Land Registry has come up with the goods.'

'Let me see,' shouted Dawn Rudd, sprinting across the room. 'Donovan, call the Armed Response Unit and tell them we're leaving immediately. Myers, your negotiation skills are needed now!'

Jemima and Broadbent were almost at the door when Dawn Rudd turned her attention to them. 'Stay here. I'll let you know as soon as we have any news.'

'Not bloody likely. We're coming with you,' said Jemima.

'No, you're not. This is my turf, my rules. I'm not prepared to risk you compromising this operation.'

'It's not up for debate. We're coming with you!' countered Jemima.

'I really don't have time for this,' snapped Rudd, shaking her head in despair. 'OK, here's the deal, you can come, but you stay well away from the cottage and you don't interfere with me or my team. I don't want to see either of you within fifty metres of the property.'

CHAPTER 33

A convoy of six police vehicles and two ambulances sped along narrow country lanes. The sharpness of bends allowed little time or room to correct the steering. Jemima had elected to drive, and she brought up the rear of the fleet.

After almost twenty minutes of Jemima's driving skills being tested to the limit, she breathed a sigh of relief when she saw that the road up ahead was blocked by a patrol car. They were about fifty metres from an isolated cottage, with the nearest neighbouring property a hundred or so metres behind them. The lead car had driven straight past the cottage, blocking the access to it on the far side.

Jemima watched Dawn Rudd step out of her vehicle. As she stared at the property she saw that there was a light on in a downstairs room. Even from that distance she could see that the curtains were closed, making it impossible to ascertain how many people, if any, were inside. Jim Stanley, the leader of the Armed Response Unit, had swiftly deployed his men around the property. Jemima had overheard him telling his team to establish any useful information which would help them determine what they were up against, along with identifying routes of access so that they would be aware of any potential means of escape.

Jemima and Broadbent waited in silence, straining their eyes as they tried to second-guess what was happening up ahead. She was finding it hard to allow a group of strangers to take over, but as this was out of their jurisdiction, there was no choice but to let the others get on with it.

While they waited, Jemima decided that she hated the countryside. Having always been a city dweller, it seemed such an alien landscape, especially at night. The darkness felt unsettlingly palpable. Far above, stars appeared like pinpricks of light but were too small and distant to be of any use. Jemima longed for street lights, garish neon signs and groups of revellers staggering about, disturbing the peace. At least in the city, you knew what you were up against.

In the distance, or perhaps it was close by, there was the occasional whisper, the rustle of foliage and something that sounded like the scuttle of tiny feet. The air was filled with the noticeable aroma of wildlife and bark.

'I've had enough of this,' said Jemima. 'Let's get closer.'

'They told us to stay back,' said Broadbent.

'And what're they going to do to us if we don't? This is our case, and I'm fed up with them treating us like a couple of naughty kids. We need to know what's going on up there.' Jemima began walking up the lane, and Broadbent followed a couple of paces behind.

Moments later there was the sound of approaching footsteps. It was a junior officer sent to tell them that there was an unlocked door at the rear of the property, with no other accessible routes of escape. 'Come and stand with the rest of us, but keep quiet so that Rudd doesn't get wind you're there,' he suggested.

Jemima and Broadbent stood amongst a group of officers. They were a few yards back from the formidable Dawn Rudd, who seemed unaware of their presence.

'My men are in position and ready to go. What do you want us to do?' asked Jim Stanley. Unlike the others, the ARU team were equipped with night-vision goggles.

'Get inside and get it done,' said Rudd.

'Have you received clarification on the number of perpetrators and hostages? We need to know exactly what we're dealing with before we breach. I don't want to put my team at risk.'

'No definite information. Likely perp—' began Jemima.

'I thought I told you both that I didn't want you anywhere near the property,' snapped Rudd, as she spun around to face them.

'It's our bloody case,' said Jemima.

'Which happens to be on my turf.'

'And right now, I'm in charge,' growled Jim Stanley. 'So stop the pissing contest and tell me what I need to know.'

'The only certainty is that a white female, early thirties, was snatched, possibly by a white male in his forties,' said Jemima. 'He's extremely dangerous and has killed before. There may be another woman of a similar age inside. What's unclear is whether she's a hostage or working with the perpetrator.'

'I want this situation resolved peacefully, so I hope that no one's trigger-happy,' said Rudd. Jemima thought it was an unnecessary attempt at stamping her authority on the operation.

'We're professionals, not a bunch of amateurs, Detective Inspector,' replied Stanley. 'Assuming there are two perpetrators, what are their names?' he asked, turning his attention to Jemima.

'Byron Toombes and Lisa Randall.'

Moments later, his voice blared out over a loudspeaker. 'Byron Toombes, Lisa Randall, this property is surrounded by armed officers. Put down any weapons you have and exit the building using the front door of the property. Walk slowly. Come out with your hands above your head. Take five steps from the door, then lay face down on the ground. Once you are in that position lace your fingers behind your head, and spread your legs apart. You must follow my instructions to guarantee that no harm will come to you.'

They waited and waited, but there was no sign of any movement from inside the property. Stanley repeated the warning, but as before, there was still no sign of movement inside the cottage.

'We're going to have to force an entry,' said Stanley. 'I want this resolved quickly and safely.'

He gave the order, and four of his men entered the building, splitting into teams of two to cover both floors of the property. Some vehicle headlights had been switched on, as the element of surprise was no longer an issue. As they waited, Jemima had to keep telling herself to breathe. As she glanced at Broadbent, she noticed he was biting his nails.

All of a sudden, Stanley cocked his head like a dog who had just heard a sound. He put a hand to his earpiece. His stance tensed as he listened intently to the information being relayed. 'Get the paramedics in there now!' he ordered.

Jemima swallowed hard as she fought the urge to vomit. It seemed obvious that Violet had been hurt. She had let her down again. She watched in surprise as Stanley spun round to face Rudd. There was no mistaking the man's fury as he squared up to her.

'You've made us look like fucking idiots!' he bellowed. 'How could you have got it so wrong? If the press gets hold of this, they'll have a field day. Our jobs could be on the line, for Christ's sake.'

'What's happened?' yelled Jemima. She was sick with fear.

'It's the wrong property! She's led us to the wrong house.' As he shouted the damning accusation, he prodded Dawn Rudd in the chest, forcing her to stagger backwards.

'That's enough!' ordered Jemima, as she forced herself between them. Tensions were quickly escalating as the blame game began. But as far as Jemima was concerned, all that could wait. The objective was still the same. They needed to find the right building and rescue Violet. 'We can't afford to waste time on recriminations. There'll be plenty of time for you two to slug it out, but right now we must find Violet Watkins!'

'What happened in there?' asked Broadbent.

181

'My team went in and scared the shit out of some old codger. He was sat inside, listening to music on his head-phones. Until they burst into the room, he had no idea that they were inside his house. He's taken it badly. He pissed him-self and started gasping for breath. Hopefully the paramedics will be able to stabilize him then take him to the hospital.'

Jemima looked away and a plaque on the gate of the property caught her eye. She marched over, bent down, and took a closer look. 'This is Primrose Cottage, not Rose Cottage!' she shouted.

'You what?' shouted Stanley, rushing across to take a look. 'Oh, you've gotta be kidding me.'

'Why didn't your men notice that sign?' Rudd asked accusingly.

'It wasn't part of our brief!' Stanley retaliated. 'You led us here. We relied on you to get your facts straight. I assure you, DI Rudd, I'm not going to let you lay any blame for this debacle on my doorstep. You should have double-checked your facts before you asked me to order my men to enter the premises!'

'If you lot are the best your force has to offer, it doesn't say much,' muttered Jemima, shaking her head in despair.

Up ahead, an officer said something unintelligible into his radio then shouted across to the paramedics. He quickly returned to the police car, got in and moved it so that the ambulance could edge forward. Another paramedic ran ahead towards the house, lugging her equipment.

Dawn Rudd paced up and down the lane as she shouted down the phone at someone in the Land Registry. 'It isn't good enough! You've just put an old man's life at risk. He could die as the result of us acting upon information that came from your department . . . I don't want to hear your excuses, just give me the correct information! A woman's life depends upon it, and I'm sure you don't want to be respon-sible for two deaths in one night!'

Rudd repeatedly tapped her pen on the bonnet of her car as she waited for the Land Registry official to give her the information she needed. When it came through, she wrote down the address and repeated it back to the person who was on the other end of the phone line. 'And are you sure that the information's correct this time?' she asked.

Jemima stood within earshot, listening expectantly. It seemed as though they had new information to go on. There was suddenly a glimmer of hope. The chase was back on.

Rudd called the various members of the team together. She told them that the Land Registry had confirmed that another property in the area was also registered to Lisa Randall, though the excitement soon waned, as when they entered the address into their GPS system, they discovered that it wasn't recognized.

'We've got to find Rose Cottage somehow,' Rudd said. 'We can't afford to waste any more time. It can't be far from here. We'll have to search the lanes. Follow along behind us, Jim. And when we finally locate the place, make sure that your men don't scare any innocent pensioners this time.'

CHAPTER 34

It was almost twelve hours since they had been made aware of Violet's abduction, and it had been twelve hours of hell for Jemima. The case had got to her in a way that no other had. It made no sense for Toombes to go after Violet again when there were so many other women he could target. He'd have known that he would be at the top of the list of any suspects, so why take the risk? Why was he so fixated upon Violet?

'You'll have to drive. I'm so angry I'd probably end up steering into a ditch or crashing into a hedge,' Jemima told Broadbent.

He knew better than to argue with her when she was in this mood. As the police convoy set off once more, Jemima and Broadbent brought up the rear. Driving along a country lane was a far cry from negotiating the roads that had led them to the police station. Broadbent did his best to keep up, but it wasn't long before the other vehicles had disappeared out of sight.

'Can't you go any faster?' asked Jemima.

'You take over if you think you could do any better,' snapped Broadbent.

'I wasn't suggesting I could.'

'Let's face it, we're on a hiding to nothing, and that fucker's going to kill her,' said Broadbent, slamming the palm of his hand against the wheel.

'Stop! Reverse back about twenty yards,' yelled Jemima.

As Broadbent hit the brakes, tyres squealed, and the car skidded to a halt. The rest of the convoy were long gone, racing ahead on their quest to find Rose Cottage.

'Back up, back up!' yelled Jemima.

'Why? What have you seen?' asked Broadbent, as he clunked the gearstick into reverse.

'There! There! It's a small track,' said Jemima. She pointed at a gap in the hedgerow, barely wide enough for a vehicle to pass. It was exceptionally narrow and almost impossible to spot unless you were purposely looking out for it, as it was obscured by a bend in the road. 'We've got to check it out. The others have missed it. They were going far too fast. It was sheer luck that I spotted it.'

'You seriously want us to go down there?' asked Broadbent. It was clear from the way he challenged her decision that he thought it would be a waste of time.

'Why not? We've nothing to lose. They're so far ahead of us. If they turned off at any point, we'd never find them. And let's face it, after the circus we've just witnessed, I don't think they've got a clue where they're going.'

As they drove slowly down the track, branches slapped against the sides of the car.

'Surely no one lives down here?' said Broadbent. 'Who in their right mind would put up with having to travel along a track like this?'

'I'm beginning to think you're right, but it's not as if we can turn round. We're committed to going forwards. We'll have to keep going until the track widens out.'

'I hate to say I told you so. Hey, is that light over there?' asked Broadbent.

'I dunno, I can't make out anything because of these hedges,' said Jemima, as she squinted in the direction he had pointed. 'Yes! Yes, it is,' she shouted.

The track veered to the left. It set them off in the direction of a property. Even from this distance, it was clear that someone was at home.

'Cut the lights,' ordered Jemima.

'Are you kidding me? I can't see a bloody thing.'

'Well if you keep them on, they're going to see us coming. We'll have lost the element of surprise,' said Jemima.

'We don't even know it's the right place.'

'That's true. In that case, it's best to leave the car here, and we'll walk the rest of the way.'

'But—'

'No buts — we'll walk. If this is where Toombes is holding Violet, then we need to get in there before he realizes we're on to him. Don't forget your taser. We're taking no chances.'

'Yeah, right. What planet are you on? Taking no chances indeed. These tasers only give us one shot,' said Broadbent. He swallowed hard, realizing that his hands were shaking. It didn't bode well for successfully deploying a single-use weapon where accuracy was imperative. 'Toombes very nearly finished me off the last time. I don't want to give him the opportunity to finish the job. I've got a wife and kid to think about. I'd like to see Harry grow up and have kids of his own.'

'We've both got kids, Dan. I want to be there for James too. God knows the lad's been through so much already. But we have to do this.' She steeled herself. 'Because of the way things turned out the last time, we've built Toombes up into some sort of super-human adversary, but he's not. He's just another lowlife who fights dirty. Though, I admit he's cleverer than most of the scum we come up against.

'Think of it this way, we're better equipped to face him this time around. Back then, you could hardly have called us partners. Let's face it, we didn't even like each other, let alone trust each other. Whereas this time around, we know each other's playbook and we're both confident of having each other's back. We can do this. And we need to do it now.'

'But we're going in there with just a taser,' countered Broadbent.

'Which is more than we had the last time. I know a single shot weapon isn't ideal. But with our wits about us and a bit of luck on our side, that should be all we need.' Jemima did her best to keep her voice light. She was absolutely aware of the inadequacy of the weapon. Especially when going up against someone as formidable as Toombes. But this was all they had, and she had a sickening feeling that, for Violet's sake, they couldn't afford to wait for backup of any kind.

As they continued on foot along the track, they soon arrived at a gate with a wooden sign attached to it. Jemima used the torch facility on her phone to illuminate it, and her heart rate increased as she read the words 'Rose Cottage'.

Their luck had changed. They had finally reached their destination.

CHAPTER 35

Jemima stared at the light in the distance. The night was so dark that she was unable to see anything other than its brightness. They needed to get closer to establish the layout of Toombes's bolthole. Jemima was sure that he would have planned for their arrival, and there would undoubtedly be some unwelcome surprises waiting for them inside the building.

'Call for backup,' ordered Jemima, as she set off towards the cottage. Seconds later, she heard hurried footsteps behind her and turned to find Broadbent. 'Are they on their way?'

'We're so far out in the sticks that we may as well be on another planet. There's no signal around here. The phones don't work, neither does the radio, so it's just you and me.'

'Well, that'll have to do because we can't afford to wait. Violet could be dead or dying in there. We've got to take Toombes down and get her out. No half measures or concerns about reasonable force. We go in hard. Agreed?'

'I suppose so. Though, I'd have felt more confident if we had the ARU to face him down,' said Broadbent.

'Me too, but they are God knows where. So there's just the two of us.'

'At least we've still got the element of sur—'

'Shit,' hissed Jemima, as a movement sensor caused a security light to illuminate the entire area. They were like rabbits caught in headlights — the only characters on an otherwise empty stage.

Having spent so long in the darkness, the brightness of the artificial light was harsh and dazzling. There was an immediate temptation to remain still and wait for your eyes to adjust, but given the circumstances, it wasn't an option. They had to reach the walls of the cottage before Toombes looked out and saw them. If they could make it in time, there was a chance he could think it had been set off by the local wildlife. With heads down so as not to be blinded, they sprinted towards the property. It was a case of hoping for the best but fearing the worst.

'What now?' whispered Broadbent, as he pressed his body against the coolness of the cottage's wall.

The light they had seen in the distance was coming from an upstairs window. The ground floor of the property appeared to be in darkness.

'We've already tipped our hand, so we can't afford to hang about. We go in. Stay a couple of paces behind me. We'll search the ground floor first. You go right, I'll go left. If it's clear, we'll head upstairs and do the same thing.'

'But we could be heading into a trap,' said Broadbent.

'That's why we need to split up. We don't know what we're about to face, but we do whatever it takes. If Toombes overpowers one of us, it'll be up to the other one to take him down. Lisa complicates matters as we don't know if she's working with him, so we treat her as though she's hostile. Get your taser ready.'

As Jemima used her free hand to try the door, her eyes widened in surprise. It was unlocked. Such a thing would be unthinkable in an urban area, but in such a remote location, it seemed unlikely that anyone would stumble across the property by chance.

A quick search of the downstairs rooms showed them to be clear, and they wasted no time in heading upstairs.

Jemima's heart rate increased with each step she ascended. Broadbent was a couple of steps behind. Two doors led off the landing, one either side of the stairs. The first was partially open with only darkness beyond. The other was closed, a thin strip of light bleeding from each of its ill-fitting edges.

There was no way to second-guess which if any of those rooms Violet and her captor occupied. The natural inclination was to think that they would be in the lit area, as they'd spotted it in the distance before Toombes would have been aware of their presence. Though it was equally possible that the light could have been left on as a ruse, and Byron could be hiding in the darkened room, which would allow him an element of surprise.

Broadbent breathed deeply and headed towards the darkened room. Jemima took the other. She stepped forward and reached for the handle, gripping her taser even tighter as she readied herself to deploy a disabling shot.

Jemima felt the blood pounding in her ears, which made it challenging to listen out for other sounds. It also didn't help matters that her heart rate had ratcheted up to an unhealthy level. Every nerve ending in her body tingled in anticipation of the inevitable confrontation. She flung the door open and rushed into the unknown. As her eyes darted about, the first thing she spotted was Violet's unconscious form, secured to a bed frame with various metal restraints.

Jemima realized they would not be able to make a quick getaway. They would need cutting equipment to free Violet from the bed frame. It took a matter of seconds for Jemima to scan the remainder of the room, and in that small amount of time, she heard a muffled sound. As she spun around to see what was happening, she was hit by a taser.

Jemima did her best to deploy her own weapon, but her body wouldn't cooperate. She was powerless as her lips parted and stretched in an ugly rictus grimace. Knowing the inevitable was about to happen, she still tried to defy the odds. Even as she willed herself to press the trigger, her arm dropped, heavy and useless as her hand spasmed, sending her own taser tumbling to the floor. She knew her plan had come to nothing. It was over. She'd failed. There was nothing she could do to protect herself now. She was helpless. And as an excruciating pain radiated throughout her body, her legs gave way, and she fell to the floor, hitting her head on the metal bed frame as she went down.

* * *

The next thing Jemima was aware of was a sharp pain in her ribs that left her gasping for air. As she struggled to open her eyes, everything was blurry and indistinct. She sensed an object hurtling towards her as a foot kicked her abdomen. Jemima cried out in agony and brought her knees up to her chest. As she blinked away the fuzziness, she saw the outline of her attacker. It took a few moments for her to realize that it was Lisa, not Byron, who was standing over her.

'I hope you've learned a lesson,' said Lisa. 'You had no right to come into my home uninvited. You're an intruder, and I'll do whatever's necessary to protect myself.'

Jemima saw that the door to the bedroom was now barricaded by a large chest of drawers. She had no idea how long she'd been unconscious. Still, it must have been at least a few minutes, as manoeuvring such a substantial piece of furniture into place would not have been quick or easy.

'Where's my partner?' croaked Jemima.

'Last I saw of him, he was out for the count in the guest room. I hope he doesn't bleed too much. It's a new duvet. I s'pose it wasn't a fair fight . . . well, hardly a fight at all. He couldn't see me in the dark, and I was ready for him. One little swing was all it took. He went down like a sack of spuds and was obliging enough to supply me with a taser. I'd never fired one before, so that was fun. Of course, it helped that you knocked yourself out.' Lisa turned away, retrieved something from the top of the chest and lowered herself on to an old-fashioned rocking chair close to the bed.

Due to the effects of the head injury, Jemima was reluctant to look directly at Lisa, as the constant movement of the seat made her feel slightly nauseous. But she knew that she had to overcome this, as she needed to concentrate on the woman.

As her strength began to return, Jemima scooted up, leaning heavily against the wall. She looked around. There were only three of them in the room.

'She's still breathing,' said Lisa, as though she was able to read Jemima's thoughts. 'But not for long. I didn't go to all this trouble just to keep her alive.'

'Why did you bring her here?' asked Jemima.

'Why'd you care about that whore?' asked Lisa.

'She's not a whore.'

'The sensible option would be to keep your opinions to yourself. In case you hadn't noticed, I hold all the cards. And it'd be better for you not to upset me. You've come here knowing fuck all about anything. Everything that's happened is her fault. Not mine. You don't know what I've been through. How could you?'

'I know that you're married to Byron Toombes. So where is he?' asked Jemima, doing her best to keep her voice low and even.

'There is no Byron Toombes. He changed his name after you lot tried to fit him up. I only ever knew him as David Randall, and he was the love of my life.'

'So where is he? Where's David?'

'David and I aren't together, but when this is over, it'll be different. We'll be reunited.'

'That's not going to be possible, Lisa. When we get out of here, you're going to have to stand trial for what you've done.'

'Shut your fucking mouth! You don't have the power to do anything. There's no way that I'm going to prison. You don't get it, do you?'

'Get what?' asked Jemima, though she already had a feeling that she wasn't going to like the answer.

'None of us are leaving this room alive. This is it. This is where it's finally going to end. David will be waiting for me, and we'll be together for ever.'

'He's dead?'

'Yeah, and it's all her fault,' said Lisa, as she picked up the large knife that had rested on her lap, and drew the blade across Violet's cheek.

Jemima looked on in horror.

CHAPTER 36

Jemima hadn't had an opportunity to get close to Violet. Lisa had told her that she was still alive, but Jemima didn't trust anything the woman said. All she knew for sure was that Violet was unnaturally still, and if the lack of response to the recent knife wound was anything to go by, it didn't seem too hopeful that she was still alive.

As for Broadbent, if Lisa were to be believed, then he wasn't in a good way either. There was no sound coming from elsewhere in the house, which suggested that he was either unconscious or dead. Jemima knew that if he was still able to move, he'd do everything in his power to help her.

As for her own plight, what concerned Jemima most was that she was only able to take shallow breaths. It suggested that her ribs were broken. The irony of Lisa attacking her in almost exactly the way that her husband had six years earlier was not lost upon Jemima.

It was all Jemima could do to sit on the floor, propped up against the wall. Her head hurt like hell, and when she tentatively reached up to touch her scalp, she found it was damp and her hair matted. She glanced at her fingertips and saw that they were stained red. Jemima knew that a head injury could be serious. She'd already lost consciousness for an indeterminate period. Her vision was blurry and she felt nauseous.

In her current state, the odds of Jemima overpowering Lisa were well and truly stacked against her. Lisa had two weapons and was fully mobile, whereas Jemima could barely see straight and felt as weak as a kitten. Once her strength returned, she would have a better chance, so the only sensible thing to do was to bide her time and try to get Lisa talking. The more recovery time Jemima had, the stronger she would become. If Jemima could develop a rapport with her captor, there was a possibility that Lisa would drop her guard. Even if it was only for a second or two, Jemima might stand a chance of overpowering and disarming her.

Before Jemima had a chance to say anything, Lisa spoke. 'You shouldn't have come to rescue her. Violet doesn't deserve it. You think she's the victim just because she's cuffed to that bed? Well, she's not. *I'm* the victim. My life's been turned upside down. I never wanted any of this. That filthy whore ruined everything. I was happy until she blew my world apart.'

'What do you mean?' asked Jemima. If she could establish what Byron had told Lisa, there was a possibility that she could sow a seed of doubt in Lisa's mind.

'That bitch corrupted him. She did things no self-respecting woman would do when people were watching. She's nothing but a dirty slut.' As the accusations tumbled from Lisa's lips, she became more emotional and her body tensed under the strain.

Lisa was already displaying signs of volatility. If she went on the attack again, Jemima was in no fit state to take her on. She needed to bond with Lisa and calm her down. If she could keep her talking, there was a chance that Dawn Rudd and the ARU would eventually locate the cottage.

'Lisa, you've got my attention. Tell me about you and Byron. How—'

'His name was David! He was always David, never Byron!' shouted Lisa.

'Yes, I'm sorry. I didn't mean to distress you. It's obvious that David meant so much to you.'

'He meant everything to me. He was my world.'

'So where did you meet?'

'The British Virgin Islands.'

'I've never been to the Caribbean, but I imagine it's quite a romantic location.'

'It's much the same as anywhere. It depends on where you are and how much money you have,' said Lisa, shrugging her shoulders dismissively. 'I'd been there for the best part of two years before David turned up. I worked in a bank over there, and he walked in one day. The moment I saw him, I had this strange feeling that we were meant to be together. You'll think its clichéd, but our eyes met, and we both knew.'

'I don't think it's clichéd at all. I think it's the most romantic thing I've ever heard. You were lucky. It doesn't happen like that for many people. So why was David there?'

'He had an account there. He came from a rich family — we're talking multi-millionaires. His parents had investments and property portfolios throughout Europe. He was an only child, his parents had died, and he'd inherited the lot. That's why he was there. He'd already changed his birth name. He'd always hated it but kept it as it meant a lot to his parents. David was his middle name, and Randall his mother's maiden name. He came to the bank in person to provide the relevant documentation for the account to be updated. It just so happened that I was the one to sort it out for him.'

'Fate pushed you together,' said Jemima.

'Exactly, we were meant to be together.'

'How long was it before you were married?'

'Oh, it was a whirlwind romance. We got engaged on our third date. Four weeks afterwards, we were married at David's mansion. It was magical. There was no expense spared. I felt like a princess, and he made me feel that way every day we were together.'

'Did you set up home on the island?'

'We'd spend November to April there each year, and travel around for the rest of the time. David needed to keep an eye on his investments. He said that there was only so much that could be done remotely. So we'd hop between the capitals.'

'The capitals?'

'London, Rome, Paris and Berlin.'

'Not Cardiff?' pressed Jemima.

'Of course not, David hated that city. He said it held such bad memories for him.'

'Why was that?'

'He'd lived there for years, working as a scene-of-crime officer. Not that he needed to work. It was an ambition of his. But in the end, it just got him down. He reached the stage where he couldn't stand seeing the aftermath of so much death and destruction. He realized it wasn't good for his mental health and decided to walk away and concentrate on his family's business interests.'

As Jemima listened to what Lisa was saying, she studied the woman's body language and facial expressions. Jemima realized that Lisa believed what she was saying. From Jemima's previous encounters with Byron Toombes, she had first-hand experience of how manipulative and convincing the man could be. It seemed that he had employed those same tactics throughout his marriage. Consistently omitting and airbrushing away any damning details from his past.

Jemima quickly appreciated that Lisa believed that her husband had changed her life for the better. It was a belief reinforced by the sudden introduction of substantial wealth and a resultant jet-set lifestyle. Throughout their time together, she would have experienced things which, up until that point, she could only ever dream about. As such, it was doubtful that Lisa would ever be open to the possibility that Toombes was not the real-life "Prince Charming" she believed him to be. 'How and when was your husband taken from you?' asked Jemima.

197

'He's been dead for two years, three months and thirteen days. It was such a shock. We were walking down the street hand in hand, not a care in the world. The next thing I knew, he let go of my hand, ran into the road, and was hit by a lorry. I was pregnant with our first child. We'd just found out that we were having a boy. I lost the baby, too — eleven days later. I went from being the happiest woman alive to having nothing apart from wealth. And I can say from bitter experience that it's true — money can't buy you happiness. I'd give it all away in a heartbeat if it meant I could have my David back.

'No one should have to suffer the way I have. It's been more than two years, yet I still wake up each morning and forget he's not there. I reach out to touch him, and when I realize he's not lying next to me, it's like losing him all over again. The grief doesn't go away. You'd think I'd have got used to it by now, but I haven't. Each time it happens, a part of me dies too. I've forced myself to carry on living, but every second of every day has been a battle. The only thing that's kept me going is the thought of making her pay for what she did to us.' Lisa turned and jabbed Violet in the ribs.

'I'm so sorry, Lisa, I can't begin to imagine what it must be like for you,' said Jemima, and she meant it. Through no fault of her own, this woman had lost everything. It had clearly driven her to the edge. But no matter how unhappy Lisa was, it did not excuse any of her actions.

'You're right, you've got no idea. I've nothing left to lose. I'm a husk. Any goodness in me died, along with David and our child. I don't feel anything apart from loneliness, despair and hatred. When she killed my husband and my baby, she destroyed me as well. But I don't see you wanting to lock her up.'

'I don't understand why you believe Violet is responsible,' said Jemima.

'That bitch was the reason he ran into the road. If it wasn't for her, he'd still be alive, and I wouldn't have had a miscarriage. We'd be a family, and we'd have been happy.'

'I don't want to add to your pain, but what exactly happened?' pressed Jemima.

'We'd flown back to the UK and were staying at our home in London. We were shopping for baby clothes. We were just walking along when David shouted out her name and ran into the road. He didn't stand a chance. The lorry hit him and tossed him up in the air. They said he died immediately.'

'I acknowledge the fact that Violet isn't a popular name, but what made you think that she was the person he had seen?'

'I didn't know at first. David had never mentioned anyone named Violet. I thought that I must have misheard. But after the funeral, I was sorting through items in his London home office and stumbled across those filthy recordings of her. I had no idea who she was at first. After months of getting nowhere, I eventually hired a private investigator. I told him to do whatever it took. Money was no object. It took him ages. I was starting to give up hope when he finally managed to track her down.

'He sent me photographs of her which confirmed he'd found the right person. She was living in Bristol at the time of David's death, but I was told that shortly afterwards she'd moved to Cardiff. I had her address, and I knew where she worked. So I decided to get myself a job there, as it would allow me to get close to her.

'I felt sick the first time I saw her in the flesh. You see, we look so similar. People even said we could've been sisters. It made me realize that's probably what David saw in me too. Her hair's lighter than mine, and her eyes are a different colour, which explains why he encouraged me to dye my hair and wear coloured contacts. I was the next best thing. The closest he'd get to her. Can you imagine how that made me feel?'

'You must have been angry.'

'Oh, I still am. It made me feel sick. David betrayed me. I loved him so much, and I thought he loved me too. I'd have done anything for him, yet he obviously didn't feel the same way about me. That slut had turned his head and made sure that I was always going to be the consolation prize. My relationship with David was everything to me, but our marriage turned out to be a sham. How stupid was I? You'd think I would have realized . . . but I didn't. I was blinded by love, and the silly thing is, I forgive him. I know you'll think I'm pathetic, but I still love him. I want to be with him.

'She's responsible for ending David's life. So I'm gonna take hers. It's the only justice I'll get. Whatever anyone says, I know it's proportionate. It's a life for a life. And then I'm going to kill myself too. I'll finally be with my David. I'll have proved to him that I'm the better woman, the only person that would lay down her life—'

There was a sound from outside, and Jemima saw the door shudder as someone tried to open it.

'Tell them to back off, or I'll end this now,' hissed Lisa.

'Guv? You OK in there?' asked Broadbent.

Jemima had never been so pleased to hear Broadbent's voice. 'We're fine, Dylan,' she said. 'Wait for me outside. I'm just chatting with Lisa. We've things to sort out and need to be left alone.' She knew that Broadbent would realize that she had purposely called him by a different name. The only reason she would have done that was to let him know that Byron Toombes was not in the room with her, as Toombes would have known his name. But the very fact that she was barricaded inside the bedroom meant that Jemima was either incapacitated or else Lisa had a weapon. And if it was the latter, then it had to be something more deadly than a taser. She hoped that Broadbent would realize that he needed to go and get help. Under normal circumstances, she wouldn't have doubted Broadbent, but she knew that he must've been unconscious for quite a while. Whatever head injury he'd sustained could very well hamper his ability to think straight and do what was necessary.

Having listened carefully to what Lisa had said, there was no doubt in Jemima's mind that the woman was completely unhinged. Discovering that her husband was not the man she had originally believed him to be must have tipped her over the edge. For some inexplicable reason this woman had fallen for Toombes and had built him up to be her Prince Charming. Given the extent of the man's apparent wealth and the fairy-tale lifestyle they had led, it was understandable that Lisa felt betrayed. She'd realized that instead of being the love of his life, she'd just been Byron's consolation prize.

Instead of picking herself up, dusting herself down, and using her new-found wealth to make a fresh start, Lisa had set out to get what she perceived to be the ultimate revenge.

'Right, time's up,' said Lisa.

The woman's voice shook Jemima out of her reverie.

'I can't sit around here all day. I'm not stupid. I know your partner's going to go for help. There's not a lot he could do by himself, and he certainly can't call anyone from here. There's no landline and no mobile signal. I'd say there's an hour tops before someone bursts through that door. But it'll be too late. It'll all be over by then.'

Jemima was surprised at how matter-of-fact Lisa appeared to be. She clearly had no intention of leaving there alive. For Lisa, it was about taking back control by doling out a fitting punishment for the so-called love-triangle that had brought about the end of her marriage. She had played the long game to reach this point, and all that remained was to murder Violet and take her own life.

It took little imagination to appreciate that neither Jemima nor anyone else would be able to talk her down. Lisa would do whatever it took to prevent Jemima from getting in the way, and if that meant killing her too, then so be it. As with Beth, Jemima would be acceptable collateral damage.

Jemima knew she needed to think clearly and act decisively to stand any chance of getting out of this situation alive. She had to focus her mind and shut out her fear. Weakened by her injuries and unarmed, the odds were stacked against her. The stakes had never been higher. She couldn't afford to make a mistake. Jemima knew how things would play out if she failed to stop Lisa. The knife was a deadly weapon, and the taser was a considerable problem too. If Jemima got zapped again, it would undoubtedly disable her. She planned to goad Lisa into firing the taser when the woman was less in control of her emotions, as it would reduce the chances of her aim being accurate. With the taser deployed, it would be one less thing for Jemima to worry about. But to do that Jemima needed Lisa's focus to be entirely upon her. The only way she could think of doing that was to antagonize her and ramp up the pressure until Lisa lost control.

'What I don't understand is that if you wanted Violet dead, why go to all the trouble of bringing her here? You could have killed her when you killed Beth. Yet you didn't. You drove all that way. It was a tremendous risk to take. And even when you arrived here, it must have taken an enormous amount of effort to get her up those stairs. What that says to me is that you didn't want to kill her.'

'You know nothing. I'm going to kill the bitch, and you're not going to stop me. The reason I didn't do it straight away is that I wanted her to regret what she'd done. She toyed with David's affections and dropped him when it suited her. If you'd seen those recordings of her flaunting herself in front of him—'

'You're wrong. Violet didn't consent to those recordings. She—'

'Of course she did. How else would—'

'She didn't. Your husband bugged some of his properties, Lisa. He targeted vulnerable young female tenants. Violet was one of them. But it was worse for her because she was unfortunate enough to have moved in next door to hi—'

'Liar!'

'I'm not lying, Lisa,' continued Jemima. She kept talking as she slowly began to raise herself up from the floor. With her back pressed to the wall for support, Jemima was able to keep her eyes on her adversary's face. She needed to move slowly and stopped in a crouched position to give her legs a chance to bear her weight. She also didn't fancy her chances of immediately adopting an upright stance. She was uncertain of how it would affect her equilibrium, as her head injury had the potential to throw her off balance. 'He stalked and eventually raped her. He also murdered her grandmother by caving her head in with a rolling pin. I worked on the case back then, and know for a fact that he made far more recordings than you've seen. We found a whole stash of them beneath the floorboards in his bedroom. He placed cameras in bedrooms and bathrooms — locations where he could spy on women when they were at their most vulnerable.'

Jemima sensed the inevitable backlash coming and needed to ensure that she gave herself a fighting chance. As she straightened her legs, her knees cracked like rounds from a shotgun. The stiffness in her limbs was a disadvantage, but the period spent on the floor had given her body time to recover. Jemima was an accomplished kick-boxer, and in one-on-one combat she was confident that the odds were in her favour.

'Liar! Liar! Liar!' screamed Lisa, her face contorting. Spittle sprayed in all directions as she vehemently defended her husband's honour. 'If you had any proof, you would have arrested him. He would have gone to prison.'

The transformation in the woman's appearance was rapid and extreme. Lisa was incandescent with rage, and her eyes gleamed with demonic fury. The rocking chair dipped forwards as she pressed down upon its arms to enable her to stand. It was a clumsy movement, as she also needed to ensure that she kept hold of both the knife and the taser.

'We'd arrested him and were taking him back to the station when someone rammed our car. It gave him time to escape, and we couldn't find him. The sick bastard went on to rape Violet and murder her grandmother,' countered Jemima. Her tactic was working, and she was determined to continue to ramp up the pressure in the hope that Lisa would make a mistake.

'He wasn't capable of doing any of those things. My David was gentle. He wasn't a violent thug.'

'Oh, he was violent all right. Face it, Lisa, your husband was scum. He certainly wasn't the man he made himself out to be. He was a sick pervert who got off watch—'

'Shut your fucking mouth!' Lisa was trembling with rage.

It took a lot of nerve for Jemima to stand her ground. There was no going back now. She was all too aware that the slightest misjudgement could end her life. The bedroom allowed little space to manoeuvre. There was no margin for error. A few millimetres either way could mean the difference between life and death. There would only be one opportunity to redress the balance of power.

The room began to feel unbearably hot as the tension between the two women boiled over. Jemima knew that she couldn't afford to let up. She continued to throw insult after insult at Lisa. 'Your husband was nothing but a sick pervert who got off watching women. No self-respecting woman wanted him. You must've been the first female to have sex with him without expecting payment in return. Were you really that desperate? Couldn't you get yourself a decent man?'

Jemima saw the slightest lowering of the knife. It wasn't much, but, combined with a noticeable tensing of the other forearm, she realized that Lisa was about to fire the taser. 'But I bet you were a disappointment. He must've closed his eyes and thought of Violet whenever he fucked you.'

The insults were too painful for Lisa to hear. It was what Jemima had been counting on. As Lisa's finger pressed down on the firing mechanism, Jemima dived diagonally forward. She knew the impact would hurt her ribs, but she was out of options. The bare floorboards were smooth enough for her momentum to allow her to swing her legs around and kick Lisa's out from under her.

CHAPTER 37

As she'd thrown herself to the floor to avoid the taser, Jemima had been unable to protect her ribs. Ideally, she would have avoided such a move, but there had been no way around it. She needed to get the knife away from Lisa, but her head injury was affecting her vision. In close combat, a millimetre either way could be the difference between life and death, and she was not the sort of person to go quietly. It made her even more determined to dig deep and give it her all.

So far, Jemima had read the situation correctly. Lisa's first mistake had been to allow Jemima to rile her. She'd fired the taser in anger, missed, and was now left with only one useful weapon. Admittedly the knife had the potential to be lethal, but as far as Jemima was concerned, her odds of coming out on top had improved considerably.

As her feet flew out from under her, Lisa fell forward. Her hands went out and she dropped the knife. There was a sickening thud as she landed heavily on one of Jemima's legs.

White-hot pain shot through Jemima's body. Her foot twisted sharply, though there was no sickening crack to accompany it. She momentarily closed her eyes and swallowed hard as she stifled a yelp, determined not to let on that she was hurt. A sprain, though both painful and debilitating, was preferable to a broken ankle.

It seemed that luck wasn't on Jemima's side. If Lisa had only landed a few inches to the right, she would have missed her entirely, and Jemima would soon have had the situation under control. As it was, things had suddenly become a whole lot more complicated. Her plan to disarm Lisa had relied upon complete mobility, and Jemima doubted she'd be able to put sustained weight on the ankle. It meant that her speed and agility were both severely compromised.

The only thing in Jemima's favour was that the knife had landed far enough away to be out of reach of both women. Suddenly, everything hinged on who had the most strength and determination to subdue the other.

Jemima needed to free her trapped leg from beneath Lisa's body. She was under no illusion that it was going to hurt like hell, but once again, she was going to have to rise above the pain. She needed to overpower Lisa before the woman had a chance to retrieve the blade.

Jemima had expected Lisa to take a few moments to recover, but as Jemima grunted and struggled to push herself up, Lisa's knee dug mercilessly into Jemima's ankle. The pressure she was applying to the injured spot was almost unbearable.

Jemima refused to give in, despite the pain being so severe that it made her see stars. She roared in defiance, reinforcing the self-belief that she was a battler, not a quitter. The sentiment spurred her on. She reached out and grabbed a handful of Lisa's hair, deftly twisting strands through her fingers to ensure that Lisa was unable to pull away. Jemima yanked her arm down as fast as she could.

As Lisa struggled to resist the downward motion, hair ripped from its roots, but she seemed oblivious to the pain. 'I'm gonna kill you,' she snarled.

The women's faces were so close that Lisa's spittle sprayed across Jemima's face.

Lisa's eyes darted about until her gaze settled upon the knife. Jemima knew precisely what the other woman was thinking, and was determined not to allow her anywhere near the blade. She wanted this confrontation to end, but that wasn't going to be possible until she had overpowered Lisa and ensured that she was unable to hurt or kill anyone. With that in mind, Jemima swiftly brought her free leg back and kicked out as hard as she could. Her foot slammed into Lisa's knee.

Lisa shrieked and momentarily eased up before driving her fist into Jemima's face. Jemima felt the cartilage in her nose shatter as blood spurted out in all directions. It seemed that no matter how hard she tried, Jemima was the one who kept coming off worst.

Lisa lurched sideways, stretching out, reaching for the knife.

Jemima slammed a fist into Lisa's throat. It was a merciless manoeuvre, but Jemima didn't care. Lisa spluttered and gasped for breath. The fight had gone out of her.

Jemima allowed herself a small, triumphant smile as she pushed the woman aside and forced herself on to her feet. It was far too painful to put much weight on her injured limb. As she limped across the floor to take possession of the knife, Jemima glanced down at Lisa. The woman had rolled on to her side. She was holding her throat, rasping noisily as she fought to drag air into her lungs.

Satisfied that Lisa no longer posed an imminent threat, Jemima hobbled towards the chest, where she hoped to find something to restrain her with, but every drawer was empty. As she scanned the room for something suitable, her eyes came to rest upon the curtains. They were old and flimsy but would have to do. Jemima just hoped that the material would be strong enough to do the job.

Jemima hobbled towards the window as quickly as she could, wincing each time her injured ankle was forced to bear her weight. With the knife in one hand, she reached up with the other and tore the curtain from the plastic rail. Miniature clouds of dust puffed into the air as successive hooks snapped.

As the curtain dropped, Jemima heard a faint sound. She turned her head and realized that the noise was coming from Violet. It was the first sign that the young woman was still alive, and Jemima almost wept with joy. But there was much to be done if Jemima was going to get both of them out of there alive. Violet was barely moving, and Jemima had no idea what injuries she had sustained.

Jemima resisted the urge to take a closer look at Violet. That would have to wait. Her immediate priority was securing Lisa before she was able to launch another attack. She turned back to the curtain, but then she heard another sound.

As she turned her head, she realized that Lisa had somehow made it on to her feet and was about to launch another attack. Just like that, Jemima's hard-won advantage was lost. Lisa was clearly not prepared to give up.

'Hands against the wall!' ordered Jemima.

'Not happening,' growled Lisa, as she quickly side-stepped to the far side of the bed. She grabbed Violet's throat and started to squeeze.

Jemima was aghast. She had expected Lisa to come for her instead of Violet. Unless she managed to stop her, Violet was going to pay with her life.

There was no hope of Violet putting up a fight. The restraints had seen to that. She was spread-eagled, weak and defenceless. It wouldn't take much effort to kill her.

Violet gasped and thrashed about as her windpipe was crushed by Lisa's hands.

'You'll have to kill me if you want to save her. Though I don't fancy your chances!' yelled Lisa.

Jemima didn't have the luxury of time. She had to act immediately if Violet was to stand any chance of survival. She changed her grip on the knife handle to hold it like a javelin, and drew her arm back, lengthening it to its full extent, before hurling the knife as hard and as fast as she was able to. As her weight shifted on to her injured ankle, she screeched in pain.

As soon as the knife left her hand, she hurled herself towards the other side of the bed. She had no idea whether the blade had hit Lisa, but Lisa continued to strangle Violet.

Jemima grabbed the trailing end of the curtain, and using both hands, twisted the material until it was taut. She was still moving as she looked across and saw that her aim had been accurate. The knife was sticking out of Lisa's chest about an inch below her clavicle. An ugly bloodstain was spreading out around the blade, but Lisa remained focused on her task.

Jemima opened her arms, reached up and slipped the length of material around Lisa's neck. She pulled backwards and downwards as savagely as she could.

Lisa struggled as Jemima crossed her hands and tightened the material around her neck. At last her hands loosened their grip on Violet's neck.

Jemima was tiring. Every moment spent on her feet was taking her a second closer to when her ankle would inevitably give way. She needed to end the confrontation once and for all. So, telling herself that it would only be a moment of excruciating pain, she kicked the back of Lisa's leg, forcing the woman on to her knees.

'Lie on your side,' ordered Jemima, as she forced her foot into the small of Lisa back.

Jemima had no idea whether Violet was still alive, but until she'd ensured that Lisa would no longer pose a threat to either of them, she had no intention of checking on her.

As Jemima secured the final knot that hog-tied Lisa, she heard sounds of voices and approaching footsteps. The knife still remained embedded in Lisa's chest.

'We need paramedics in here!' she shouted, as tears of relief ran down her cheeks. 'You'll have to force the door. There's a chest jammed against it, and I've done my ankle in.'

Despite being empty, the chest of drawers was so heavy and sturdy that the rescue team were unable to force the bedroom door open. In the end, someone had to take an axe to the door.

Even though she was hog-tied, Lisa still struggled against her restraints, seemingly unconcerned about the knife still embedded in her flesh.

EPILOGUE

Jemima later learned that Broadbent had been knocked unconscious the moment he had stepped into the darkened bedroom, as Lisa had been waiting in the shadows, ready to attack whoever came within range. When he eventually regained consciousness and realized that he was unable to do anything to assist Jemima, he set off in the car to try to get help. He had had the foresight to activate both the siren and the blue flashing lights, which was how Dawn Rudd's team had located him so quickly.

Jemima and Broadbent were taken to hospital with Violet and Lisa. Apart from a couple of stitches, Broadbent's injuries were superficial, but Jemima was found to have three broken ribs, a badly sprained ankle, a head wound that required six stitches, and a broken nose.

While recovering in hospital, Jemima found out that, after extensive surgery, Lisa had been saved. She was then assessed by a psychiatric team, who concluded that she should be sectioned under the Mental Health Act. She was charged with one count of murder, together with abduction, false imprisonment, a further attempted murder, GBH and ABH. She would serve out whatever sentence she was eventually given in a secure mental health facility.

Remarkably, Violet had also survived the ordeal. She had been placed in an induced coma for a few days to allow her horrific injuries to start to heal.

When Violet had recovered sufficiently to be able to give them an account of what had happened, she told the police team that she and Beth had got into Lisa's car when she had stopped to offer them both a lift. It had been raining heavily when they got off the bus, and as Lisa was a work colleague neither woman sensed that she was a threat. Violet's final memory of that evening was Lisa offering them coffee from a thermos. The half-empty flask was discovered in Lisa's car, and when its contents were tested, it was found to have been laced with GHB.

Violet confirmed that when she regained consciousness, she was disorientated. The effects of the drug impaired her memory, and the fact that she was blindfolded had heightened her terror, as she had no idea what was happening. It had taken a while for her to realize that she had been restrained. Lisa had remained silent as she doled out a series of sadistic punishment beatings.

Lisa had finally removed the blindfold when her desire for information had grown too great, and it became necessary for her to speak. She was eager for Violet to cooperate and desperate to hear what she had to say about the man Violet had known as Byron Toombes. Lisa had questioned Violet for hours, physically attacking her whenever Violet said something that contradicted Lisa's imagined view of what had happened all those years earlier.

The medical staff insisted that Jemima remain at the hospital until the afternoon, as they were concerned about her head injury. She had spoken to Kennedy on the telephone, and he assured her that he would send an officer to collect her.

It was four o'clock and still no one had arrived. Jemima was about to pick up the phone and ring Kennedy again when she heard the sound of some familiar voices. At first she thought that it must be her mind playing tricks on her, but moments later her father and James strode into the ward.

'Jem!' squealed James, running towards her.

'What're you doing here?' she asked, trying not to cry out as he threw his arms around her.

'We've come to take you home,' said James, snuggling into her.

'I thought you were going to the Carmichaels' this evening?' said Jemima, glancing up at her father.

'Oh, I never wanted to go in the first place. It's more your mother's sort of thing. Anyway, I had somewhere far more important to be. I had to bring my grandson to pick up his brave mum.'

Jemima began to sob.

'What's the matter? Are you hurt? Do you need a doctor?' asked James.

'No, I don't need a doctor. These are happy tears, James,' said Jemima. She kissed his cheek and reached out to squeeze her father's hand.

* * *

When a case ended, it had become something of a tradition for the squad to gather at a local pub and enjoy a few drinks. It was a few hours' downtime when they'd kick back and cast off responsibilities, which for much of the time weighed heavily upon their shoulders. They'd commandeer the dartboard, shoot some pool and generally have a laugh.

Theirs was a profession where, regardless of rank, the pressure of the job was always present. No two days were ever the same. Some were mundane, though that was rare. Others were like wading waist-deep through a sea of treacle, doing your utmost to reach the shoreline, while being buffeted from every possible direction. Those shifts were demoralizing. You worked your guts out only to find that you'd made little or no progress. But the hardest to deal with were those occasions when split-second decisions were required and lives depended upon you making the right call

But if you called it right, the subsequent buzz was nothing short of elation.

The sojourn to the pub had been delayed while Jemima and Broadbent were recovering, but they had finally all been able to get together.

Jemima was struggling to enjoy herself though. She couldn't shake off the feeling that they'd let Violet down. If they'd ensured that Byron Toombes had faced a trial by jury, it was likely that he wouldn't have gone on to have a relationship with Lisa. Back then, they had more than enough evidence to guarantee a conviction. As a murderer, rapist and stalker, he would have faced years behind bars.

'Huxley, turn that frown upside down. That's an order!' barked Kennedy, as he handed her a fresh drink.

'Sorry,' she muttered half-heartedly. Her lips barely curled into a forced smile before she gave up trying and raised her glass to take a sip.

'I've known you long enough to know what you're thinking. Put aside whatever misplaced guilt you're feeling,' continued Kennedy. 'Remember, we worked that first case together, and I'm telling you we did everything we could. There's no comeback on any of us. You and Daniel are a pair of fine officers who go above and beyond. No one could have predicted what happened this time around. But the important thing is that you dealt with it. Let's face it, you went out on a limb. If you'd left it to that mid-Wales lot, Violet would have ended up dead. End of.' He slammed his fist on the table to emphasize that he was right.

When the dartboard became free, they headed over to begin the usual squad tournament. After each round, the weakest player dropped out, until only two players were left. Jemima was knocked out first and Broadbent was eliminated in the second round. Shaking his head in defeat, he ambled over towards Jemima, who was perched on the edge of her seat, nursing a drink.

'What's up?' he asked, as he sat next to her and nudged her arm.

'Nothing really.' Her voice sounded far from convincing.

'Come on, it's me you're talking to. Something's not right.'

'You'll think I'm stupid.'

'I doubt that, so spill.'

'Do you remember me telling you about that feeling I had?'

'About someone watching you?'

'Yeah, that's the one. Well, it hasn't gone away.' Jemima raised her eyes and saw the concerned expression on Broadbent's face.

'So what's happened?'

'Nothing I can put my finger on. It's just a feeling that someone's watching me.'

'What's this?' asked Kennedy, dropping on to one of the free seats. Having been eliminated from the latest round, he was happy to sit and talk.

'Noth—' began Jemima.

'Tell him, or I will,' said Broadbent. His tone left no doubt that he was serious.

'Dan's making something out of nothing,' she said.

'She thinks someone's stalking her.'

'You what?' Kennedy's arm stopped abruptly, sloshing beer over the rim of the glass. Some of the liquid landed on his shirt, but he seemed oblivious of the fact.

'I wouldn't put it that strongly. I've just got a feeling that someone's watching me.'

'She mentioned it when we were trying to find Violet,' said Broadbent.

'Exactly, it was probably linked to Toombes,' said Jemima, trying to downplay the whole thing.

'No. You're not getting away with that. You told me back then that you'd had the feeling for a while, and I told you that you needed to trust your gut. There has to be something to it if you're still feeling that way.'

'Daniel's right. Specifics, lady, now! You've upset a hell of a lot of people over the years. It's not beyond the bounds of possibility that some lowlife's got it in for you.'

'But I can't tell you anything, because nothing's actually happened. It's just a feeling. I'm probably just being paranoid.'

'You're sure about that?'

'Positive.'

'Well, you stay vigilant. And remember, we're here for you,' said Kennedy.

'I know. Now can we just get back to enjoying ourselves?'

'Oooh yesss! Champion! Champion!' yelled Gareth, holding his arms aloft.

'You may want to cut that celebration short, lad. I think you've forgotten, the winner buys the next round,' laughed Kennedy.

THE END

ALSO BY GAYNOR TORRANCE

JEMIMA HUXLEY CRIME THRILLERS
Book 1: THE CARDIFF KILLINGS
Book 2: THE BRIARMARSH CLOSE KILLINGS
Book 3: THE CAERPHILLY MOUNTAIN KILLINGS